STREET
FOOD

STREET
FOOD

Rani King and Chandra Khan

PIATKUS

For Dad

Dodwell Francis Cooray 25.9.14–20.1.97

From our first shuddering breath when you held us close, through our first faltering steps when we clung on to your finger for support, to the wise and soothing counselling you gave as our grownup hearts were broken, you were always there, our father, our friend, our mentor.

Though we cannot talk or laugh or walk with you today, we know we shall be with you again tomorrow.

Thank you Dad for giving us what little talent we possess and the self-confidence to succeed that only comes from knowing we were totally loved, valued and cherished.

And for Mum left behind – funny, heroic, loving, exasperating, adorable – who has always loved us with the fierce protection of a mother tiger.

© 1997 Rani King and Chandra Khan
First published in 1997 by
Judy Piatkus (Publishers) Ltd
5 Windmill Street, London W1P 1HF

A catalogue record for this book is available from the British Library

ISBN 0 7499 1750-4

Photographs by Steve Baxter
Food prepared by Oona van den Berg
Styling by Marian Price
Text designed by Paul Saunders
Step-by-step illustrations by Rodney Paul
Decorative artwork by Paul Saunders

Typeset by Phoenix Photosetting, Chatham, Kent
Printed and bound in Great Britain by
Butler & Tanner Ltd, Frome, Somerset

Contents

Acknowledgements

Rani especially thanks her life-support of close friends who have listened, encouraged, praised and generally made her feel like a jolly good (and amazingly clever and talented!) human being. As always, her darling boys Justin and Julian (the centre of her universe and the best sons a mother could have) and 'adopted' daughter Caroline.

Also Geoff and Sylvia Bobker, Helen Hague and John Steel, Julia Soave, Jackie Dane, Mike Boland, Rose Spittles, Oyinkan Olakunri and the Department for Education and Employment for being a great employer. Not forgetting for one moment Heather Rocklin our much-loved editor, and all our friends at Piatkus Books (long may our association continue!), Mark Lewis, Peter Irvine and Henry Harris at Harvey Nichols and everybody connected with our weekly TV series *Flavours of the Orient* on Granada Sky. In your own way you have made our success just that bit sweeter because of the love and delight you have shown at our progress. Thank you.

If **Chandra** thanked everyone who gave her a shoulder to cry on, laughs on the way and a jolly good telling off when she needed it, she would have to publish an entire book of acknowledgements! Those who particularly deserve her gratitude are 'brother and sister' Laddie and Mary Khan, Bev and Carl Hinds, Terri Herbert and her girls, Linda, Toni, Marcia, Carol, Ramila and Margaret and not forgetting Annette Lento who always makes her feel clever and important. Thanks and love to you all.

Introduction

WELCOME to this guide to *al fresco* eating from the streets of South-East Asia – Tiger Lily style!

All the recipes in this book can be easily recreated in your own kitchen. The key is simplicity, absolutely fresh ingredients, and very fast cooking which will in no way detract from the sensational flavours of these vibrant dishes. We do hope they will transport you to the teeming street markets of the East, full of the unique aromas of some of the best food in the world!

We are very excited about this book because it gives us a chance to revisit places we remember visiting in the past, and share some of our favourite recipes with you. These have been adapted from Thai, Indonesian, Sri Lankan and Malaysian dishes, with the odd Caribbean one thrown in for good measure (Chandra's husband John is from Guyana). All the recipes have been inspired by the many wonderful food sellers – 'hawkers' – who ply their trade on the streets and waterways of South-East Asia.

Those who live their lives under mostly grey and cloudy Western skies (as we do now) can only share in our most vivid culinary memories for a few short summer months. At the first sign of pale watery sunshine, barbecues are dragged out of hibernation, and later (often) charred offerings are handed out on paper plates, accompanied by lukewarm wine and wilting salads. Oh dear!

Why not discover food purpose-made for sunshine eating – and enliven even the dullest winter day with a splash of colour and the delight of an exotic, delicious meal?

The world is shrinking, as package holidays allow more and more people to visit countries which used to be but a distant dream. Even in Britain a recent survey showed that rice and curry is now the nation's favourite meal, beating wonderful roast beef and Yorkshire pudding into second place (and this before the mad cow scare put many people off eating beef!).

The interesting and fresh cuisine developing in Australia, heavily influenced by its Balinese, Thai and Indonesian neighbours, is rapidly gaining credibility, while every restaurant or pub in the UK now seems to have a South-East Asian flavour to their menu. Our company, **Tiger Lily – Oriental Fire**! – is building up an excellent trade supplying world-class chefs with our instant mixes and spices – reflecting their clients' growing demands.

Oh, to be in climes where the sun shines nearly all the time and a bountiful harvest from land, sea and sky simply begs to be turned into delicious meals! Eating on the streets becomes a way of life. In South-East Asia, and Sri Lanka (our homeland), eating out is an everyday occurrence.

In Thailand some 80 per cent of the population do not even have a kitchen. But why slave in a hot and steamy kitchen when hawkers come out like stars at night? Whether served from the deck of a floating restaurant or a modest *sampan* in Thailand, or by itinerant cooks on bicycles, how we remember those delicacies we loved to eat back home!

During the day all sorts of food can be bought from the many traders who start work at a time when you or I would still be tucked up in bed. Because of the ferocious heat after midday (remember the old song about only mad dogs and Englishmen going out in the noonday sun?), work and school start very early – about 7 a.m. On rising, a cup of tea will usually suffice. Later in the morning, friends often gather at local *kades* (eating huts) to pass the time of day and indulge in soup rice, clear soup noodles with perhaps some pork and greens, stringhoppers, hoppers, or *thosais* (savoury pancakes) with coconut *sambol* and fried fish. Or they might take some floury *char sui* buns from a vendor's huge bamboo container which would be steaming on a street corner, sending forth its enticing aroma.

Lunchtime in Sri Lanka would see many bicycle men weaving through the traffic, their panniers holding precariously stacked plates tied in cloth squares or metal 'tiffin carriers' – all containing freshly made rice and curries. These would be delivered to those unwilling to leave the safety of air-conditioned schools and offices. Hometime (from 1.30 to 3.30 p.m.) meant escaping from the heat of the city and having a quick snooze under slowly rotating fans, or in the garden on a hammock under rustling palm trees, before waking up to a cold refreshing shower and sauntering out for a bite to eat.

But it is at night that South-East Asia comes alive and street traders really come into their own.

Under a huge tropical yellow moon and skies lit by a million twinkling stars, the balmy night air begins to fill with the maddening aroma of sizzling barbecued pork soaked in soy sauce and painted with a mixture of honey, cinnamon and lime juice. We remember the 'slap slap' of pastry being tossed on high and stretched to make tissue-thin *roti canai* or *mutarba*, filled with spicy curry. In Penang, Singapore and Kuala Lumpur the streets throng with entire families. Everywhere, one hears the bubble of cauldrons of soup noodles, the hiss and sizzle of food cooked over glowing embers and the cacophony of noisy chat and milling crowds.

We remember music of all kinds, from *bailas* (a rumba-type dance brought to Sri Lanka by the Portuguese) to Jim Reeves, Acker Bilk and Elvis. It was wonderful to sit by the harbour in Penang or Colombo watching the waves break and reluctantly retreat, before returning to pound the beach again. Large flames from flares stabbed into the earth would light our meals – hot, fragrant and sometimes served on banana leaves.

As if it was not enticing enough, having all this food within a short distance of our home, it even arrived on the doorstep! Our Uncle Gerald and Aunty Sumana lived on the borders of Bombalapitiya and Colpetty (a suburb of Colombo, the capital of Sri Lanka), a short distance from the Suans' Dragon Café which we loved visiting. Invariably, halfway through the evening as we sat out on the verandah, we would hear the 'ding ding' of the *godamba roti* man's bell. He would ride a customised bicycle with a simple aluminium box (not unlike a large square biscuit tin) attached. Inside was a small spirit burner which heated the surface of the box until it was hot enough to cook the *rotis* on. He would take a small piece of dough and, within minutes, transform it into a huge gossamer-fine piece of pastry by flipping it into the air.

When we were sure the *roti* was so fine it would fly away, he was finally satisfied and would cook it on the hot box, turning and throwing drops of coconut oil over it. Rani's special favourite was egg *roti* – for this he would break a whole egg on the pastry, which was folded over and over until it formed a square parcel of many layers, interleaved with cooked omelette.

From nowhere he would spirit up *seeni sambol* (a sweet and hot onion relish) and a fish or meat curry, and we would eat this with our fingers, breaking off the flaky layers to mop up the spicy juices.

And all this for a few rupees.

Our memories of barbecues are of digging deep pits in the sand. We would line them with seaweed, place large stones on the fire built at the bottom, add more seaweed and then toss in lobsters, crabs and clams (killed first), cover them with more seaweed and wait impatiently until the smell started our tummies rumbling in anticipation. We enjoyed these impromptu meals in Sri Lanka, and then in the USA, where we would catch crabs ourselves as children, in Chesapeake Bay, Maryland.

Our very dear family friend, Uncle Jaya, would lie on a floating airbed, with his face pressed against the transparent window set in the pillow. When he saw a particularly fine specimen, he would charge us to go after it. Despite our anxiety about crab nippers so near our exposed toes on the sea bed, we eagerly pursued them. The taste of those freshly steamed crustaceans, with dripping hot sauce or butter oozing down our arms and chins – what bliss!

If you have already met us by reading our first book, *Tiger Lily – Flavours of the Orient*, you will be familiar with our family story. If not, let us briefly tell you about our wonderful childhood. Our father was a Sri Lankan diplomat and our mother a Chinese film star. They met in Malaya when Dad (then a cub reporter on the *Malay Times*) was sent to interview Mum when a film of hers was released in Kuala Lumpur.

She spoke no English: he no Chinese. And for the first year or so of their married life they communicated in sign language. They married, with the disapproval of both parents. Mum's father (Kung Kung, as we were taught to call him, although we never met him) was a rich and influential member of the last Emperor's court. He had five wives and twenty children and Mother was his favourite. When she married Dad she sent home the customary wedding photo of them pictured cheek-to-cheek.

By return came an elaborately tied red parcel. This traditionally held money and the deeds to property and houses. Instead, Mother's side of the photo fell out, with Dad carefully cut off and torn into a thousand pieces. The accompanying letter berated her for moving to a 'slave country' (Sri Lanka, or Ceylon, as it was a dependency of Britain) and marrying a 'black devil' to boot. Dad's parents were equally disapproving, so they married in a registry office with a can of beer and no cake, and spent their wedding night on a rush mat on the floor of a friend's house.

Fifty years later we arranged a special wedding ceremony officiated by our Minister friend Elaine Jones. Mum, carrying a bouquet of golden-coloured flowers, walked up the aisle to beaming Dad, to the strains of 'Here Comes the Bride'. Another friend, Rosalie Waldock, sang 'Ave Maria' with the voice of an angel. We were bridesmaids and held a slap-up reception for over 200 guests and the 'newly-weds' even went off on honeymoon! As Mum said, 'All these years I feel we have been living in sin – now I feel we really *are* married.'

Our first memories are of living in the grounds of a royal Thai palace. Rani was born there. These were superb days – Dad was with the UN and we had servants and a care-free existence. When Ceylon won its independence from Britain, Dad took us back there and joined the Diplomatic Corps. After several more idyllic years living in an island paradise, he was posted to the UK and the USA.

We were very fortunate that our parents, unlike other diplomatic families, took us everywhere with them, rather than sending us off to boarding school. Our travels may well have disrupted our formal education but how much we gained: visiting art galleries and historic sites throughout the world; mixing with people from different cultures and backgrounds; and, of course, eating our way around the globe.

As you can imagine, we ate in many wonderful restaurants and grew to love food with a passion that has not diminished over the years.

We do hope you will enjoy trying out the recipes in this book. Please don't be afraid to experiment and adapt them to your own taste. After all, that is what we have always done! The short cuts we use will help you recreate the exciting taste of street food quickly and easily in your own home.

For the many of you who have written to us saying how much you enjoyed our first book, *Tiger Lily – Flavours of the Orient*, and our anecdotes about our families, here is a brief update. This past year has changed our lives forever. Our first book was launched at a champagne reception with oriental buffet at Harvey Nichols's chic Foundation Bar and Café with its wall of running water, festooned with tigerlillies. We were delighted to see a crowd of journalists, friends and family and none prouder than our much-loved parents. They both stood, frail and leaning on walking sticks, in the front row while we publicly gave tribute to the love, care and encouragement we have always had from them. Dad had tears in his eyes and his chest was out, bursting with pride. He wore a tigerlily in his buttonhole and a jazzy multi-coloured silk waistcoat while Mum looked like a little doll in her golden wedding dress. Everybody loved them.

Three months later we buried Dad in the same outfit. He had suffered a massive heart attack in a restaurant after a good steak lunch. He died, laughing and joking and planning his next holiday to Sri Lanka, in Chandra's arms. John and Mum were also at his side. Elaine came back to Holy Trinity to conduct the service and once more Rosalie used her beautiful voice to uplift us with 'Ave Maria'. Dad's six grandsons carried him into the church to the sounds of Louis Armstrong's 'Hullo Dolly', while Neisha walked him in carrying our traditional white umbrella and we all contributed to the service in a packed church. We took him back to his beloved homeland in March and we shall always be grateful for the years we had of this talented, modest, gentle and loving man. His final work was to edit this book for us.

And what of the rest of the family?

Justin, Rani's eldest, and his girlfriend Caroline have bought their first house and are busy redecorating. Neisha, Chandra's firstborn but our 'shared' daughter, is becoming more involved in the family business. Rani's youngest, Julian, refuses to be depicted as the 'village idiot', as he says he was in the last book, and will therefore be carefully checking this book ('Why was Justin made out to be the clever one?')! Johnny, Chandra's youngest, is forsaking his image as the fast-food junkie of the family and learning to eat and make recipes from our first book.

John, Chandra's husband, is getting used to stepping into the breach and can now label, pack orders, and produce daintily wrapped gift baskets as well as us. He and Chandra are looking forward to a world cruise when Tiger Lily finally repays all the years we have devoted to it, whilst Rani? Rani is supremely confident that around the corner will be an entrepreneur willing to back our chain of fast-food noodle/rice restaurants (to rival Macdonalds and KFC!). Oh, and of course the good-humoured, loyal, fascinating millionaire who will whisk her off to a tropical sunset . . .

Mum is overwhelmed by the response we have had from the media, and is not so quietly proud of her 'little girls'. And as for us – well we are trying to keep our feet on the ground, following appearances on Radio 4's *Woman's Hour*, Sky TV, Granada, BBC radio, etc, etc – oh, and our own three-times-a-week series of half-hour cookery programmes called *Flavours of the Orient* on Granada Sky TV!

We hope you will enjoy this book and please do keep writing in – we love hearing from you.

Storecupboard Ingredients and Basic Recipes

T HERE ARE a few essentials that you will need before you start using this book.

The essential tools are a pestle and mortar or electric coffee grinder, a liquidiser, some sharp knives and a wok or deep-fryer.

In the East our trusty pestle and mortar (usually made of stone) acts as a grinder, liquidiser and blender. We use it to pulverise ingredients such as whole spices, chillies, ginger and garlic. In the West, with the variety of machines available, we would suggest that whole spices are ground in a coffee grinder, sauces and liquids are achieved with a blender/liquidiser, food processors could be used for fine chopping and making pastes, while garlic could be crushed with a traditional garlic crusher. If a recipe requires minced ginger, an ordinary cheese grater does the job extremely well.

If you can afford it (and they are now very reasonably priced from catalogue stores like Index or Argos), we strongly advise you to invest in an electric rice boiler. The sheer bliss of automatic rice cooking will free you to experiment and banish forever grainy uncooked kernels or stodgy 'pudding-type' disasters.

STORECUPBOARD INGREDIENTS

The storecupboard ingredients are divided into two groups: essential items needed to concoct great-tasting meals; and optional extras, to make the recipes taste even more authentic.

Essential

ginger; garlic; soy sauce (we tend to use the darker variety as it is stronger); hoisin sauce; sugar (dark brown or white); salt; vinegar (we always use malt); oil (any vegetable oil or peanut or sunflower but *not* olive oil); black or white pepper; sherry (sweet or dry but we usually use sweet); fresh chillies (remove the seeds for less heat – we prefer to leave them in); ground chilli, coriander, cumin and turmeric; cinnamon sticks; cloves; sesame oil; coconut milk (powdered or in a can); creamed coconut (in a block); onions; Heinz tomato ketchup; chilli sauce (preferably Encona hot pepper sauce); crunchy peanut butter; cornflour; chicken stock cubes (Knorr is best); ground mixed spice.

Optional

dried prawns; chickpea flour (*besan*); runny honey; ginger wine; galangal; lemon grass; curry leaves; pandanus leaf (*rampe*); kaffir lime leaves; straw oyster mushrooms; dried tamarind (in a block); shrimp paste (*blachan*); fish sauce; jaggery (palm sugar); maldive fish; dried wood ear Chinese mushrooms; five spice powder; whole cardamom pods; *tung choi* (preserved Chinese vegetable).

We usually serve all the savoury dishes (including soups) at once on or in communal dishes. Guests help themselves to what they want and eat the dishes in whatever order they like. It is not against the rules to sip the soup in between mouthfuls of rice, curry, etc. Desserts are mostly a selection of the luscious fruits that grow so prolifically in our countries. When offering any of the cooked desserts, we find it best to do so in small amounts, as they are often very rich.

Ingredients vary in strength. For example, the smaller the chilli, the hotter the taste. Chilli powder also varies in its potency. Likewise fish sauce and even soy sauce can have quite different strengths.

Faced with the problem of how much chilli to recommend you put into our recipes, we discovered a simple solution at the Indra Regent Hotel, Bangkok. Here, small bowls of different ingredients are laid out for diners. There are always chopped fresh and dried chillies, sugar, salt, fish sauce and soy sauce. Everybody just helps themselves, according to their own preferences. Why not try the same technique when serving your Oriental meal?

Barbecuing is one of the most popular ways of cooking street food in the East and just as popular in England when the weather allows! A barbecue can be as simple as a tin or clay flower pot filled with charcoal and topped with a grill or mesh, or an elaborate construction involving hoods and side tables. We prefer the simple Greek-style barbecue, a long, narrow box-like affair (with an optional small motor which rotates the spit), as the length of the container allows us to cook large quantities – absolutely essential when entertaining starving family and friends.

The art of barbecuing is waiting until the charcoal is really hot and topped with white ash (which takes about an hour), *never* using paraffin or fire-lighters which will taint the flavour of the food, and marinating your meat as long as possible (overnight is best) before cooking. This, and basting it frequently, will ensure that the dish is as tender, moist and succulent as possible. A handful of herbs thrown on the charcoal adds extra flavour. Citrus leaves, e.g. lemon or lime, are particularly delicious.

BASIC RECIPES

The very first thing we did when asked by our publishers to write this book was to book our fares to Bangkok, Kuala Lumpur and Penang. For where better to experience street fare at its best?

At every stall we ate at (how we suffered for our art!!), no matter how humble, and every restaurant however grand, we were presented with a series of different sauces. Some were so fiery hot they brought tears to our eyes – some milder and sweeter, with undertones of lemon and fish sauce.

Many of the marinades we share with you are used to soak the meat before cooking so that the lovely flavours penetrate deep into the heart, tenderising as they go.

The quick and easy way to really good Oriental and South-East Asian cooking is to make your own sauces and marinades. Set aside a weekend to make a batch and keep them in the refrigerator. Not only will you save the money you would have spent buying inferior products at inflated prices but you will have the satisfaction of making your own.

CHILLI PASTE

✦

THIS brilliantly simple paste will last for several weeks in the refrigerator. Use between 1 teaspoon and 1 tablespoon to 1lb (450g) ingredients to add a fiery taste of the Orient!

1½oz (40g) fresh chillies, green or red, roughly chopped, or 18 dried red chillies

5 tablespoons oil
3 cloves garlic, peeled and roughly chopped
½ teaspoon salt

1. If using fresh chillies, put all the ingredients in a food processor and whizz until you have a smooth paste.

2. If using dried chillies, place them in a bowl, cover with boiling water and leave to soak for about an hour or until they soften. Drain the chillies, throw away the water, place in a food processor with the other ingredients and process as before.

3. Store in a clean, dry jam jar and cover with a thin layer of oil.

ONION OIL

This is excellent for stir-frying and also for salad dressings.

6 spring onions, washed, dried thoroughly, trimmed and chopped

6 tablespoons oil

1. Heat the oil in a saucepan until smoking, then turn the heat down and simmer for 10 minutes.

2. Pour the oil over the spring onions, leave to cool and strain. (You can use the onions in any recipe which needs fried onions; just reduce the oil a little.)

3. Pour into a clean, dry screw-top bottle and keep in the fridge.

COCONUT, CORIANDER AND CHILLI MARINADE

✦

THIS perfect marriage of South-East Asian flavours turns white meats, fish and prawns into a delectable bite of Oriental heaven! Tinned coconut milk is now available from most supermarkets, thankfully. We always keep a few tins in reserve. At a pinch, it can be used instead of thin pouring cream with ordinary desserts.

MAKES enough for 1lb (450g) meat or fish

1 × 14fl oz (400ml) can coconut milk
finely grated rind and juice of 1 lime *or* 2
   stalks lemon grass, chopped
4 tablespoons chopped fresh coriander
   leaves

5 spring onions, washed, trimmed and
   roughly chopped
1–2 fresh red chillies (to taste)
2 tablespoons oil
1 teaspoon salt
1 teaspoon coarsely ground black pepper

1. Put all the ingredients in a food processor or liquidiser and blend for a few minutes until you have a smooth paste.

2. Marinate meat, fish or prawns in the mixture for at least 2 hours. Then remove from the marinade and barbecue, grill or oven bake until cooked, basting frequently with the marinade.

EASY BLACK BEAN SAUCE

✦

A DELICIOUS, Chinese-inspired sauce, excellent as a pouring sauce and can also be used for cooking spare ribs.

Salted black beans can be found in Chinese food shops, usually packed in polythene bags. As they have a rather pungent odour, it's a good idea to keep them in an airtight container, and rinse them well before use.

MAKES enough for 2lb (900g) fish, prawns, chicken or ribs

1 tablespoon salted black beans

1 clove garlic, peeled and crushed

1 small fresh chilli, chopped

½ teaspoon salt

½ teaspoon grated fresh ginger

2 teaspoons rice wine or sherry

1 tablespoon hoisin sauce

1 tablespoon vinegar

2 tablespoons oil

1 teaspoon cornflour

1 teaspoon sesame oil (optional)

1. Rinse the beans in water and drain. Put all the ingredients in a liquidiser and blend until smooth.

2. Put the mixture in a saucepan and heat gently until thickened. Adjust the seasoning, then use.

VARIATION

✦ Try adding 2 tablespoons diced red or green peppers and/or tomatoes, 1 tablespoon tomato ketchup, and 1 tablespoon crushed pineapple, to make a sweet sour type of sauce.

QUICK TERIYAKI SAUCE

✦

THIS Japanese-inspired sauce or marinade is perfect for white and dark meats but is also very good on salmon, bream or jack (also known as king) fish. A particularly easy recipe.

MAKES enough for 1lb (450g) meat or fish

1 tablespoon cornflour
4 tablespoons sherry
2 tablespoons cider vinegar

2 tablespoons runny honey
1 teaspoon ground cinnamon
9 tablespoons dark soy sauce

1. Mix the cornflour into a smooth paste with the sherry, then add the rest of the ingredients.

2. Soak the meat or fish for at least 3 hours in the marinade.

3. Grill, barbecue or oven bake until cooked, basting frequently with the marinade, to keep it succulent and juicy.

SPICY BARBECUE SAUCE

✦

PARTICULARLY good as a marinade with tuna, or with red meats like beef or lamb, this recipe can also be used as a tasty sauce. Try mashing it into a scooped-out baked potato, spoon back into the skin, top with cheese and grill for a real supper treat. Please do not be frightened of crossing continents and tastes when cooking or eating. Western food can all be spiced up with a judicious teaspoon of any of our marinades or sauces.

MAKES enough for 1lb (450g) meat or fish

1 tablespoon oil
1 large onion, peeled and finely chopped
2 cloves garlic, peeled and crushed
1 teaspoon ground ginger
1 tablespoon Jerk Seasoning (p.9)
1 × 14oz (400g) can tomatoes

4 tablespoons tomato ketchup
3 tablespoons Worcester sauce
3 tablespoons jaggery (palm sugar) or
   dark brown sugar
1 teaspoon freshly ground black pepper

1. Heat the oil in a saucepan, then fry the onion and garlic until brown.

2. Add the ginger and jerk seasoning and stir for 1–2 minutes, then add the remaining ingredients and bring to the boil.

3. Reduce the heat and simmer for 10–15 minutes or until the sauce is thick and reduced.

4. Taste and adjust the seasoning. When cool, use to marinate meat or fish for at least 1 hour, before barbecuing, grilling or baking (basting, as always, to keep the meat or fish moist). Or serve hot as a spicy sauce for barbecued meat.

JERK SEASONING

✦

AT THE end of August each year, at Carnival time, a small portion of London is magically transformed into a part of the West Indies. For three days, the streets of Notting Hill resound to steel bands, calypso and reggae music, while over a million people of all ages, shapes and colours, often in outlandish attire, 'tramp' (dance) behind the glittering floats.

Enterprising local householders hurriedly set up makeshift stalls in their gardens and sell anything edible they have in the house to take advantage of the ravenous hordes. Over the streets waft the delicious smells of barbecuing jerked chicken and pork, curried goat and *rotis*.

Jerk is a spicy seasoning originally used by the Arawak Indians of South America to flavour whole pigs which were then barbecued slowly over fires made from the bark of the allspice tree. We are more familiar today with its round berries, commonly used in cakes, which exude the fragrance of cinnamon and cloves. Although jerked suckling pig is a dish for the gods, this mixture is equally good used on small joints of meat or pieces of chicken which can then be barbecued, grilled or oven-baked. Jerk seasoning will keep for at least two months in an airtight jar in the refrigerator.

MAKES enough for 4–6 meals for 4 people

2 shallots, peeled and roughly chopped

1 fresh red chilli, roughly chopped

5 spring onions, washed, trimmed and
 roughly chopped

juice of 1 lemon

2 teaspoons ground allspice

2 teaspoons salt

1 teaspoon dark brown sugar

2 cloves garlic, peeled and roughly
 chopped

1 teaspoon chopped fresh thyme

1. Put all the ingredients in a food processor and whizz until you have a paste.

2. Keep in an airtight container in the fridge and use 2–3 teaspoons per 1lb (450g) meat. Leave to marinate for approximately 2–4 hours (overnight if possible) before cooking.

FRIED ONION FLAKES

✦

WE OFTEN try to track down dried onions in a weigh-and-serve health shop. You can just throw them into hot oil and fish them out immediately. Making fried onion flakes with fresh onions takes more time but is worth the effort. They are an essential Oriental ingredient, added to dishes or sprinkled on top as a garnish.

1lb (450g) onions, peeled
1 pint (570ml) oil

1. Slice the onions very thinly. A food processor with slicing attachment is ideal, as all the slices should be the same thickness or they will not cook evenly and some may burn.

2. Heat the oil in a saucepan. Add the onions, then cook slowly until they are deep brown, taking care that they do not burn. Slow cooking is essential to drive out all the moisture or the onions will not be crisp. Drain on kitchen paper.

3. When cold and crisp, crumble and store in the cupboard in an airtight screw-top jar.

SAUS KACHANG

Mild Peanut Sauce

✦

HERE IS a quick and easy sauce to go with Chicken Satay (p.80). *Kachang* is the Indonesian word for peanut, and there are as many recipes for satay sauce as there are satay-sellers. Satay is invariably served with chunks of cooling cucumber, raw onion and, sometimes, small, deadly hot chillies.

8 tablespoons peanut butter
2 teaspoons dark brown sugar
½ teaspoon garlic salt
3 tablespoons soy sauce

1 teaspoon shrimp paste (*blachan*),
 optional
½ teaspoon chilli powder
4fl oz (110ml) canned coconut milk
½ teaspoon lemon juice

1. Put all the ingredients in a saucepan and heat gently until well mixed.

2. Adjust the seasoning to taste, and add enough water to get a consistency that is to your liking. Some peanut butters are thicker than others; some people like their *Saus Kachang* quite runny, while others prefer to scoop it up with their satay sticks. The choice is yours!

EASY PEANUT AND ORANGE DIP

✦

WE HAVE always believed in using ready-prepared ingredients as long as they are of high enough quality. Why spend hours grinding peanuts in oil when chunky peanut butter can sit comfortably in the storecupboard to be spread on the kids' sandwiches or to make this easy dip?

3 tablespoons crunchy peanut butter
3 tablespoons orange juice
1 tablespoon tomato ketchup

½ teaspoon garlic salt
½ teaspoon chilli sauce

1. Combine all the ingredients, beat well together, and serve.
   Serve with Spicy Prawn Fritters (p.25), Spicy Fried Chicken Wings (p.77) or any type of satay.

SWEET GARLIC AND CHILLI SAUCE – 'FIVE ALIVE'

✦

SOUTH-EAST Asian cuisine relies very heavily on spicy dipping sauces. Every street vendor has a motley assortment of jam jars, old relish bottles and other containers holding a selection of homemade sauces made according to jealously guarded 'secret family recipes'. Customers ladle small spoonfuls over their meal or at the side of the plate in which to dunk spring rolls and other savouries. This versatile concoction can also be used as a marinade and a seasoning for stir-fried, grilled or baked dishes.

Very hot and utterly delicious, any surplus sauce can be safely stored in a clean jar in the fridge for up to a week.

The recipe should be easy enough to remember – five ingredients in quantities of five.

SERVES 5 (of course!); makes enough to marinate 1lb (450g) meat or fish

5 cloves garlic, peeled and crushed
5 red chillies, finely chopped
5 tablespoons hoisin sauce

5 teaspoons soy sauce
5 teaspoons lemon juice

1. Pound the garlic and chillies to a paste, then stir in the rest of the ingredients, and serve.

2. If using as a marinade, leave the meat or fish to marinate for at least 1 hour, then drain, reserving the liquid. Grill, using the marinade as a basting sauce; or stir-fry, adding the liquid (a teaspoon at a time to ensure the dish is not too fiery) during the last 5 minutes of cooking time.

TAMARIND RELISH

✦

WE HAVE always had a weakness for the sweet sour tang of tamarinds and this is one of our favourite recipes. It has been a closely guarded secret until now, as it is very similar to one of the range of relishes with which we first launched our company.

We use it as a relish, to pep up cooked dishes like pasta, and even as a marinade and stir-fry flavouring – for anything, in fact, which benefits from its unique tart sweetness. We share it with you now and hope you enjoy it as much as we do!

SERVES 6–8

4oz (110g) block of dried tamarind or 4oz (110g) concentrated tamarind
15fl oz (425ml) malt vinegar
1oz (25g) red chillies, chopped
½oz (15g) black mustard seeds
1oz (25g) garlic, peeled and roughly chopped

1oz (25g) ginger, peeled and roughly chopped
4oz (110g) raisins
12oz (350g) white granulated sugar
1½oz (40g) salt

1. If using dried tamarind, bring half the vinegar to the boil, soak the tamarind in this for 30 minutes, then squeeze well, retaining the liquid and discarding the fibrous residue. Strain the liquid before using.

2. Blend the chillies, mustard seeds, garlic, ginger and raisins with 2 tablespoons of the vinegar (adding more vinegar if required), in a food processor, until you have a coarse paste.

3. Heat the remaining vinegar in a pan, add the sugar and stir until dissolved. Add the paste and salt, and bring to the boil.

4. Add the tamarind (concentrate or the liquid from the dried), and boil gently, for approximately 20–30 minutes, until syrupy. Stir occasionally.

5. Spooned into a warmed sterilised jar, this relish will keep for at least a year.

A SELECTION OF DIPPING SAUCES AND SEASONINGS

✦

H ERE ARE some suggestions for easy sauces and seasonings. Serve them in small bowls for guests to dip their spring rolls, morsels of fish, seafood, meat or vegetables into, before popping them into their mouths. Having a selection of these sauces ensures that each bite is a unique taste sensation.

It is difficult to give precise quantities – your guests may like lashings of sauce or just the merest touch. Apart from the tomato ketchup one, the dipping sauces should be very thin and watery.

- ✦ equal amounts of Heinz tomato ketchup and Encona chilli sauce (our two favourites and no, we don't get paid to promote them!)
- ✦ soy sauce mixed with sesame seeds
- ✦ soy sauce mixed with chopped fresh chillies to taste
- ✦ soy sauce mixed with very finely grated ginger
- ✦ 2 chillies liquidised with 6 tablespoons fish sauce and 2 tablespoons oil
- ✦ fish sauce
- ✦ rice wine or cider vinegar
- ✦ white sugar
- ✦ crushed chillies
- ✦ chopped fresh garlic
- ✦ chopped roasted peanuts

Appetisers

O NE OF the most noticeable cultural differences between the West and the East is that Oriental people simply adore food and are not ashamed to be seen snacking all day long. Smart businessfolk, golden jewellery dangling, will rub shoulders with lowly road sweepers at a roadside stall, thoroughly united in their appreciation of good food! This unashamed enjoyment may have a lot to do with upbringing – the ritual of four-hourly feeding for infants would be viewed with amazement by an Eastern mother. She will breast-feed her child on demand until it is at least two years old, and will carry it around with her at all times perched on a hip. Most children seem so happy and content with this attention that they rarely suffer from eating disorders or, indeed, temper tantrums.

On the way to our luxury hotel in Bangkok from the airport, we noticed a great deal of building work going on. Amongst the hard-hatted workers trundling wheelbarrows, shifting bricks and earnestly building walls on top of an unfinished skyscraper some fourteen storeys above street level, we were very amused to see a palm-leaf-covered shack with two women underneath it madly stir-frying something delicious on a portable gas stove!

No matter what time of day it is, someone will be on every street corner offering delectable savoury titbits. Here are some of our favourites – they make interesting starters or snacks. Most will keep well in an airtight container in the fridge for a few days.

VADES
Spicy Fritters

✦

H OW WE love *vades* – the smell of hot coconut oil and the sight of these crunchy little fritters floating in it, turning an appetising brown ... When we travelled by coach in Sri Lanka, the *vade* woman or man would board the bus while we waited at the station. Balancing large flat baskets, lined with fresh banana leaves, on their heads, they would walk up and down the aisles or thrust their wares up invitingly through the open windows, in front of our twitching noses.

Our particular favourites were prawn *vades*, with one large enticing crustacean resting in the centre of each fritter. If they could talk they would say: 'Eat me, eat me!'

Serve *vades* with a dipping sauce, like Tamarind Relish (p.13), as a starter or snack. Although unconventional, a side dish of chopped onions, tomatoes and cucumbers, mixed with sugar, salt, lemon juice and chilli powder to taste, would go well and help to moisten the *vades*.

MAKES 16–20; enough for 4–6

8oz (225g) white maize flour or cornflour	1 teaspoon salt
3fl oz (75ml) yoghurt	½ teaspoon sugar
¼ teaspoon bicarbonate of soda	½ teaspoon chilli powder
2 teaspoons oil	½ teaspoon ground turmeric
2 cloves garlic, peeled and crushed	½ teaspoon garam masala
1 teaspoon grated fresh ginger	2 pints (1.2 litres) oil (coconut preferably)
2 green chillies, finely chopped	for frying

1. Mix all the ingredients together in a bowl, except the oil for frying.

2. Add 4fl oz (110ml) water a little bit at a time, until the mixture forms a stiff dough. Leave to rest in a cool place for at least 2 hours or in the refrigerator overnight.

3. Break the dough off into small balls and pat out into round discs about 1½ inches (4cm) in diameter. Wet your hands if the mixture sticks.

4. Bring the oil to smoking heat in a wok, then carefully lower in the *vades* a few at a time. Lower the temperature and fry for about 4 minutes until golden brown and fluffy, turning once. Keep frying until all the *vades* are cooked.

5. Drain on kitchen paper and serve warm.

VARIATION

◆ If liked, press a whole unshelled prawn into each *vade* before frying.

SRI LANKAN VADES

✦

THESE *vades* take a bit more time but they are really scrumptious, resembling Middle Eastern falafels. A dipping sauce made from equal quantities of tomato ketchup and chilli sauce will give them an extra kick.

SERVES 6

1lb (450g) yellow lentils or chickpeas
1½ teaspoons salt
4 curry leaves, crumbled
a 2 inch (5cm) piece *rampe* or pandanus leaf, chopped (optional)
1 teaspoon ground prawns or maldive fish (optional)
1 teaspoon ground black pepper

½ teaspoon chilli powder
½ teaspoon garlic powder
1 green chilli, finely chopped
1 teaspoon ground cumin
4oz (110g) chickpea flour (*besan*)
2 pints (1.2 litres) oil
about 24 unshelled prawns (optional)

1. Wash the lentils or chickpeas until the water runs clear. Place in a deep bowl, cover with plenty of water and leave to swell overnight. The next day, rinse with fresh water and drain.

2. Use a food processor to grind the lentils or chickpeas a little at a time, adding some water each time, taken from 4fl oz (110ml). Make it as smooth as you can, although a little texture adds to the taste. You are aiming to form a thick paste.

3. Mix in all the ingredients except the oil and prawns, and leave to rest for about 4 hours.

4. Flour a work surface with the chickpea flour and break off enough dough to make a small rissole-like patty. Roll the mixture in your hands until it forms a smooth ball, then squash it slightly. Press a whole shell-on prawn into the middle if liked.

5. Heat the oil in a wok until it begins to smoke, then carefully lower in about 5 *vades* at a time and deep-fry until golden brown (about 8 minutes, depending on their size. Drain on kitchen paper and serve warm.

OPPOSITE *Top to bottom:* Kway Teow (page 58) and Spicy Prawn Fritters (page 25)

MIXED VEGETABLE PAKORAS

✦

ALWAYS popular, these tasty titbits are munched all day in the East, in the same way as a Westerner would scoff a bag of crisps. Pakoras can be used as a starter, served with a savoury dip such as Tamarind Relish (p.13) or chopped fresh chillies mixed with soy sauce. This is such an easy recipe so be sure to keep it handy. When entertaining, make them in advance and gently warm in the oven or microwave before serving. Mmm!

MAKES 16–20; enough for 4

For the batter
½oz (10g) chopped garlic
½oz (10g) grated fresh ginger
3 green chillies, roughly chopped
1 teaspoon chilli powder
2 teaspoons salt
1 teaspoon ground turmeric
2 teaspoons ground cumin
1 teaspoon ground coriander
½ teaspoon ground black pepper
1 teaspoon vinegar
6oz (175g) chickpea flour (*besan*)

For the vegetables
1 potato, peeled and coarsely grated
4oz (110g) cauliflower, broken into small
    florets
1 medium-sized onion, peeled and
    chopped
2oz (50g) fresh spinach, washed and
    chopped
2 tablespoons cooked peas
1 pint (570ml) oil

1. Put all the batter ingredients, except the chickpea flour, into a liquidiser. Add 4fl oz (110ml) water, and process until blended. Put into a bowl, stir in the chickpea flour and keep to one side.

2. Put the potato and cauliflower into a pan with 2 tablespoons water. Bring to the boil and cook for 1 minute only. Drain and cool.

3. Mix all the vegetables with the batter, then heat the oil to smoking point in a wok. Drop in tablespoons of batter (no more than 8 at a time) and fry until brown, turning over halfway. The pakoras will float when ready and should take about 4 minutes to cook.

4. Drain on lots of kitchen paper and serve.

OPPOSITE An Oriental breakfast of Egg and Crab Scramble (page 91), Passionfruit Cooler (page 136) and Parathas served with butter and jam (page 46)

SRI LANKAN CURRY PUFFS

✦

IF YOU go to any Sri Lankan home inevitably a plate of these will be passed around. They are a bit like mini Cornish pasties, but curry puffs (or patties) are filled with a spicy mixture and baked or fried. We have adapted our national snack to make it less calorie-laden. Yummy as a starter or at teatime.

MAKES 25–30; enough for 4–6

For the filling
1 tablespoon oil
1 medium onion, peeled and finely
  chopped
3 curry leaves, chopped (optional)
8oz (225g) minced meat (beef, lamb,
  chicken or pork)
1½ teaspoons ground black pepper
2 teaspoons curry powder
1 teaspoon mixed spice
grated rind of 1 lemon
2 green chillies, chopped

1 medium potato, peeled, boiled and cut
  into small chunks
1½ teaspoons salt
1 teaspoon vinegar
1 teaspoon supermarket mint sauce
3 tablespoons coconut milk (canned or
  evaporated cow's milk)
For the pastry
2 × 1lb (450g) packets frozen puff pastry,
  thawed
flour
2 eggs, beaten

1. To make the filling, heat the oil in a frying pan, and fry the onion until it softens and begins to turn brown (and the curry leaves, if using). Add the meat, pepper and curry powder and stir until the meat begins to turn brown.

2. Add all the remaining filling ingredients and simmer until almost dry. Taste and adjust the seasoning (it should be quite spicy and salty). Leave to cool.

3. Roll the puff pastry out thinly on a floured surface. Use a 3 inch (8cm) cutter to make circles. Brush around the edges with egg, put a teaspoon of filling in the centre of each circle and fold over to make a semi-circular puff. Use a fork to press round the edges, taking care to seal them properly. Use any left-over egg to glaze the tops of the curry puffs.

4. Preheat the oven to 190°C/375°F/Gas Mark 5. Wet the baking trays with water, then pour off to leave the trays damp. Place the puffs on the trays and bake for 20–25 minutes, or until puffed and golden brown.

Chilli Meatballs

✦

THESE delicious meatballs can be served warm or cold. Dip them in Sweet Garlic and Chilli Sauce (p.12) or Spicy Barbecue Sauce (p.8) and be transported to paradise! They are good with mixed salads, pitta or naan bread; or the half-size ones can be speared on toothpicks and placed on a tray or dish with a selection of dips. They are ideal for those on a diet, especially if you make them with very lean minced meat.

Makes 12 or 24

1lb (450g) lean minced meat (beef, lamb, pork or turkey)
1 tablespoon hot chilli sauce
1 tablespoon tomato ketchup
½ stalk lemon grass, finely chopped
½ small yellow pepper, finely chopped

2 spring onions, washed, trimmed and finely chopped
½ teaspoon each salt and ground black pepper
1 clove garlic, peeled and crushed
½ teaspoon celery salt (optional)
3 tablespoons sesame seeds (optional)

1. Mix all the ingredients, except the sesame seeds, if using, together in a large bowl.

2. Divide into 12 or 24 balls and roll in sesame seeds if liked.

3. Preheat the oven to 190°C/375°F/Gas Mark 5 and bake, or barbecue, for about 15 minutes, turning once, or until brown.

INDONESIAN BARBECUED SPARE RIBS

✦

PORK RIBS are found everywhere in South-East Asia. Even in devoutly Muslim countries where pork is abhorred, Chinese butchers can be found tucked away, out of sight of the ordinary housewife.

This recipe is different from the better-known sweet and sour ribs but could well rival them in your affections. By the way, we were thrilled to discover jaggery (palm sugar) on sale in our local Oxfam shop. Now you can indulge your sweet tooth at the same time as supporting a struggling Third World community.

These ribs make good party fare. Remember to put out individual finger bowls if serving at a formal sit-down meal (we usually put out small bowls of warm water scented with a drop or two of orange or rose water, with a few petals or small whole flowers floating on top). If serving them at a buffet, put plenty of paper napkins out – these are seriously sticky, finger-licking good!

SERVES 4–5

2 red chillies, chopped
2 cloves garlic, peeled and crushed
2 tablespoons jaggery (palm sugar) or brown sugar
a 1 inch (2.5cm) piece ginger, peeled and grated
1 small onion, peeled and very finely chopped
2 tablespoons soy sauce

2 teaspoons salt
1oz (25g) tamarind pulp, mixed with 5 tablespoons hot water, then sieved, *or* use 2 tablespoons brown sauce
1 teaspoon ground turmeric
1 tablespoon oil
2lb (900g) spare ribs, cut into 2 inch (5cm) portions

1. Put all the ingredients (except the oil and ribs) in a blender and blend on high until you have a wet paste. Add water if necessary. Spoon over the ribs and turn them until they are well coated.

2. Heat a wok, then swirl the oil around and add the ribs. Cook over a low heat, adding extra water if necessary, for about 20 minutes.

3. Preheat a grill or barbecue. Then cook the ribs, turning them over occasionally with tongs until they are brown and crispy, and basting with leftover sauce.

THAI SAUSAGES

✦

A MILLION miles away from our usual beloved British bangers, these sausages are small and round, like cherry tomatoes. Try to track down sausage casings which are available from good kitchenware companies, such as Lakeland Plastics (based in Windermere), or talk very nicely to your local butcher. You will need 20 inches (50cm) casing. Those lucky enough to have an attachment on their food processor or a sausage-maker (a giant fearsome-looking syringe which churns out long lines of sausages) can make these in double quick time. Serve them with Sweet Garlic and Chilli Sauce (p.12).

SERVES 4–6

6oz (175g) ground or minced pork
2 tablespoons cooked rice
2 tablespoons lime juice
1 teaspoon finely crushed garlic
½ teaspoon ground coriander
1 teaspoon ground black pepper

½ teaspoon salt
¼ teaspoon sugar
¼ teaspoon chilli powder (optional)
1 tablespoon finely chopped fresh
    coriander leaves
5 tablespoons oil

1. Mix all the ingredients, except the oil, together in a bowl and use to stuff the skins. Tie into small balls at 1 inch (2.5cm) intervals. Chill in the fridge overnight.

2. Prick well with a fork, then fry slowly in the oil, turning frequently, until well browned and cooked through.

STUFFED FRIED CRAB

✦

THIS IS a dish we concocted using prawn shapes or crab sticks made of reconstituted prawn or crabmeat, fish and seasoning. We really love them and we often chop or mince them to add to other dishes; we don't believe in turning our noses up at new products which can make life easier. Those purists who really want to start from scratch can use fresh boiled crabs instead. If you are using sticks or shapes, you can put the mixture in empty scallop shells.

Serve them on a bed of small diced tomatoes, cucumber and onions tossed in lemon juice and sea salt, and scatter some more chopped fresh coriander over the top. Accompany with a bowl of savoury sauce – Tamarind Relish (p.13), Sweet Garlic and Chilli Sauce (p.12) or Spicy Barbecue Sauce (p.8) – and serve as a substantial starter or with white rice as a main meal.

SERVES 4

2 eggs, separated
4 × 5oz (150g) crabs (cleaned and dressed) *or*, if you want to do it yourself, 4 × 8oz (225g) crabs (make sure the gills or 'dead men's fingers' and inedible stomach are thrown away, and pick out every tiny trace of shell) *or* 1lb (450g) crab sticks or prawn shapes, chopped, and 4–6 deep scallop shells
4oz (110g) finely minced fresh pork
½ stalk lemon grass, finely chopped

1 clove garlic, peeled and crushed
½ inch (1cm) piece ginger, peeled and grated
1 teaspoon chopped fresh chives
1 teaspoon chopped fresh coriander (root, stalk and leaves)
a pinch of five spice powder (optional)
a pinch of sugar
½ teaspoon freshly ground black pepper
1¾ pints (1 litre) oil

1. Whisk the egg whites and mix with all the ingredients except the egg yolks and oil.

2. Put the mixture back into the crab or scallop shells, piling it in and pressing down firmly to compact the meat. Steam over boiling water for 30 minutes. Put aside to cool down.

3. Beat the egg yolks and use to brush the mixture in each shell, to seal. Heat the oil in a wok until smoking. Reduce the heat to medium and carefully lower in the stuffed crab or scallop shells, meat-side down. Spoon oil over the top and fry for 2 minutes until brown.

SPICY PRAWN FRITTERS

✦

THESE are utterly delicious and we found them on every street corner. No matter what slight variations each cook made (whether adding extra chillies, different spices, extra fresh coriander or minced pork), every one we tried was scrumptious – and we must confess we tried them all! Served with Sweet Garlic and Chilli Sauce (p.12) or Easy Peanut and Orange Dip (p.11), they make a terrific starter and they're also great for parties. They look even better when nestled in a bed of crisp shredded lettuce, with wedges of cucumber and tomato, and lime to squeeze over.

Rice flour is available from most Chinese and Asian stores, Harvey Nichols Food Market, and we have even found it in some supermarkets and health food shops.

MAKES about 20; enough for 4

4oz (110g) cooked peeled prawns
1 teaspoon ground cumin
2 teaspoons ground coriander
3 spring onions, washed, trimmed and chopped
1 clove garlic, peeled and crushed
½ inch (1cm) piece fresh ginger, peeled and grated

1 teaspoon salt
½ teaspoon ground black pepper
1 small chilli, chopped
5fl oz (150ml) canned coconut milk
1 egg, beaten
4oz (110g) rice flour
1¾ pints (1 litre) oil

1. Chop the prawns fairly coarsely.

2. Put the spices, spring onions, garlic, ginger, salt, pepper, chilli and a little of the coconut milk into a liquidiser and blend until smooth.

3. Add the egg, the remaining coconut milk and the rice flour to the liquidiser, and whizz until well mixed.

4. Tip the mixture into a bowl and stir in the prawns.

5. Heat the oil in a wok and fry the mixture in teaspoonfuls, not too many at a time. Fry until crisp and golden, then turn over and fry on the other side. Drain on lots of kitchen paper.

MANGO ACHARU

✦

WE WERE sent to the Methodist College for Girls (MCG) in Colpetty, mainly because our Aunty Gladys Loos was an ex-head-mistress and great-grandfather Reverend Zaccheus Nathanielsz had some connection with Colpetty Church to which it was attached.

MCG had a tuck shop, as did all boarding schools (though we were day girls – our parents disapproved of boarding). In the shop were such delicacies as fish pancake rolls, *mas* buns (curried meat rolls) and fruit in season, but our favourite was mango *acharu*, a sour pickle. We would be served small portions in paper cones, or straight into our hand from a big pot, and enjoyed licking off the last traces of spicy sauce.

Acharu should be sour hot and only slightly sweet – a very addictive taste. It is lovely used as a spicy starter or as a salsa (hot chunky sauce). Serve with small torn pieces of *roti*, papadums, naan bread or tortilla chips.

SERVES 4 as a chunky dip or salad

3 large or 4 smaller mangoes
juice of 1 lime
1 teaspoon salt

a pinch of sugar
1 teaspoon chilli powder

1. Choose mangoes that are hard, slightly green and under-ripe.

2. Skin them and cut the flesh away from the stone. Using a sharp blade, chop the flesh into small fingernail-sized cubes.

3. Mix with the rest of the ingredients and leave in the refrigerator for at least 4 hours to allow the flavours to develop.

VARIATION

✦ Try adding ½ small, very finely chopped onion to the *acharu*, adding more seasoning according to taste.

Soups

WALKING in any street in Malaysia, Indonesia or Thailand, it is unusual not to pass a vendor sitting on a garishly coloured small plastic seat stirring a huge cauldron of steaming soup. Next to the cauldron are piles of different noodles or a massive rice boiler. Tender a handful of small change (the equivalent of about 50p) and you will soon be tucking into a bowl of delicious, highly spiced soup. Most are hot, flavoursome broths in which float chunks of meat, fish or poultry topped with fried crispy onions or chillies. They are usually clear, but the Thais, Malays and Indonesians do love their coconut milk-based soups too. Sri Lankan soups are thinner and often contain lentils and tomatoes, flavoured with fragrant spices.

Wayside stalls usually specialise in one particular soup, served with noodles or rice. Each hawker uses their own secret combination of ingredients, but, whichever soup you choose, you can bet it will be very substantial: a meal in itself. Always but always you will be offered chilli, whether chopped finely and served sprinkled as a tonsil-screaming garnish, or as a paste, oil or sauce.

Soup is served at the same time as the other dishes when eating at home, and is sipped throughout the meal. As a very important part of a Thai meal, the flavours are intense, unique and delicious.

THAI RICE AND SEAFOOD

✦

A SUPERB soup full of the natural goodness of the sea, and a popular choice for lunch. To make the recipe quicker and easier, instead of the shrimps, cockles and mussels, use 8oz (225g) prepared frozen seafood which can now be found in most supermarkets.

Small dishes of sugar, crushed red chillies, fish and soy sauces and chopped salted roasted peanuts should be served with this soup-rice so that guests can season it to their own tastes.

SERVES 6

For the fish stock
2lb (900g) fish scraps (any kind)
1 stalk celery, washed and chopped
1 carrot, washed and chopped

For the soup
16 mussels (closed ones only)
1 clove garlic, peeled and crushed
a small slice of fresh ginger, peeled and grated
1 small chilli, chopped
1 spring onion, washed, trimmed and chopped

3 tablespoons oil
4oz (110g) fresh shrimps, heads and shells removed (use them for your stock)
4oz (110g) fillet of white fish (any kind), cut into bite-sized pieces
2oz (50g) cockles or clams
7oz (200g) rice
2 tablespoons fish sauce
1 tablespoon chopped fresh coriander leaves

1. If making your own fish stock, ask your fishmonger nicely for the fish scraps. Put the scraps, and the shrimp heads and shells in a pan with 3½ pints (2 litres) water, the celery and the carrot. Cover, bring to the boil and simmer for 20 minutes (*no more*). Any longer and the flavour will become 'gluey' – very unpleasant! Strain and use the liquid only. Alternatively, use 4 good-quality fish stock cubes with the equivalent amount of water, or 3½ pints (2 litres) canned fish broth.

2. Scrub the mussels and put them in a heavy iron frying pan. Cover and cook over a high heat until they open. Throw away any that refuse to open.

3. Fry the garlic, ginger, chilli and spring onion in the oil in a large saucepan, then add the fish stock and the rest of the ingredients (except the fresh coriander) and simmer for about 35 minutes or until the rice is cooked.

4. Serve in deep bowls sprinkled with the fresh coriander.

THAI SPICY CHICKEN AND LIVER SOUP

✦

THIS IS one of Chandra's favourite soups. Although none of us likes to eat liver as a main dish, in this soup it loses its strong flavour and adds an interesting depth to the chicken. The watercress or lettuce should retain some of its crispness – delicious and packed with vitamins.

SERVES 4–5

12oz (350g) raw chicken breast, cut into bite-sized chunks

4oz (110g) chicken livers, cleaned and cut into small chunks

¼ teaspoon salt

½ teaspoon ground black pepper

2 pints (1.2 litres) homemade chicken stock or 2 chicken stock cubes mixed with the same quantity hot water and 1 teaspoon sugar

2 spring onions, washed, trimmed and finely sliced

a 1 inch (2.5cm) piece fresh ginger, peeled and chopped

1 stalk lemon grass, finely chopped

3 kaffir lime leaves or the rind of 2 limes cut into very fine strips

juice of 2 limes

1 bunch watercress or ½ small iceberg lettuce

For the spicy sauce

2 red chillies

2 tablespoons sugar

2 cloves garlic, peeled

3 tablespoons fish sauce (optional)

extra lemon or lime juice (to taste)

1. Mix the chicken breast and liver with the salt and pepper and put to one side for about 10 minutes.

2. Bring the stock to a rolling boil, add the spring onions, ginger, lemon grass, lime leaves or rind, and juice, and boil for 15 minutes. Add the chicken breast and liver and simmer for a further 10 minutes.

3. In the meantime, put the spicy sauce ingredients in a mortar and pestle or a blender and grind or process until smooth, adding a little extra water if necessary. Put into a small dish to accompany the soup.

4. Pick over the watercress, throwing away any tough bits, or wash the lettuce thoroughly. Shred finely, add to the soup and boil for only 1–2 minutes until the leaves are just wilted.

5. Serve with the spicy sauce so that your guests can add just the right quantity of 'liquid fire' to suit their palates.

SOTO BANJAR
Chicken Soup with Eggs

✦

THE NAME of this soup always makes us smile – it seems to promise a rendition of 'Oh Susannah!' or 'Camptown Races' played on the banjo! In fact this is a hearty and satisfying Indonesian dish originating from Java. As always, it can be bulked up, using potato patties (see opposite), compressed rice cakes or egg noodles. It tastes great on its own, too.

SERVES 4–5

3 chicken stock cubes (Knorr is best)

1 breast of chicken or 6oz (175g) shredded meat or ham

1 tablespoon oil

5 spring onions, washed, trimmed and sliced

3 cloves garlic, peeled and crushed

3 small chillies, chopped

3 chopped kaffir lime leaves or the grated rind of 1 fresh lime

4oz (110g) Chinese cabbage, sliced

2 stalks celery with leaves, finely chopped

1 teaspoon ground white pepper

½ teaspoon sugar

4 hard-boiled eggs, cut into quarters

1. Dissolve the stock cubes in 3½ pints (2 litres) water. If using chicken, poach it in the broth until just cooked. Remove and shred into quite small pieces. Set aside the chicken, meat or ham and broth.

2. Heat the oil in a saucepan, then fry the spring onions, garlic and chillies over a low heat for 4 minutes.

3. Add the stock, the lime leaves or rind, Chinese cabbage, celery, pepper and sugar. Bring to the boil, then simmer for 10–15 minutes. Taste and adjust the seasoning.

4. Divide the chicken, meat or ham, the potato patties (if using) and the eggs between 4 large individual soup bowls and pour over the broth.

POTATO PATTIES

MAKES 8

2 medium potatoes, peeled, boiled and mashed

3 spring onions, washed, trimmed and chopped

¼ teaspoon white pepper

½ teaspoon salt

1 small chilli, chopped

1 tablespoon chopped celery

1 teaspoon shrimp paste (optional)

1 egg, beaten

1 pint (570ml) oil

1. Mix all the ingredients together, except for the egg and oil, and form into 8 flat patties. Refrigerate for at least 30 minutes.

2. Dip the patties into the egg, heat the oil in a wok or deep frying pan, and fry until golden brown.

VARIATIONS

✦ For compressed rice cakes, use an easy boil-in-the-bag rice but cook for 1 hour instead of the time specified. Leave until the rice is cold, then snip open the bag and slice the rice into 1 inch (2.5cm) cubes. Use instead of the potato patties.

✦ For noodles, add 2oz (50g) cooked egg noodles for each person and omit the patties.

TOM KHAA KAI
Coconut and Galangal Soup

✦

THIS IS one of Thailand's most popular soups: creamy, spicy, delicate and very, very delicious. Please do not be put off this recipe by the word 'galangal'. Galangal is an aromatic root similar in taste and appearance to ginger but more intensely fragrant. If you really can't get hold of it (though most supermarkets are starting to respond to the increasing clamour for Oriental ingredients), substitute ginger.

SERVES 4–6

1 × 8oz (225g) block creamed coconut dissolved in 2 pints (1.2 litres) water *or* 2½ × 14fl oz (400ml) cans coconut milk

3 spring onions, washed, trimmed and finely chopped

2 stalks lemon grass, chopped

4 small chillies, chopped

5 kaffir lime leaves *or* the rind and juice of 1 lemon or 2 limes

½oz (15g) galangal or ginger, peeled and sliced into very thin shreds

11oz (300g) raw chicken breast, cut crossways into ¼ inch (5mm) slices

7oz (200g) fresh oyster or button mushrooms, sliced

½ tablespoon fish sauce or 1 teaspoon salt

3 tablespoons chopped fresh coriander leaves and stems

1. Put the coconut milk into a pan with the spring onions, lemon grass, chillies, lime leaves or rind (not the juice at this stage or it will curdle), and the galangal or ginger. Cover and bring to the boil. Immediately turn down the temperature and simmer for 10 minutes.

2. Add the chicken and the mushrooms and bring back to the boil. Boil for 2 minutes or until the chicken is just cooked.

3. Remove from the heat, then stir in the fish sauce or salt, the lemon or lime juice if using and the fresh coriander. Taste and adjust the seasoning, and serve. Do not boil again if reheating.

HAM AND CUCUMBER SOUP

✦

IN CHINA, winter melon would be used to make this refreshing soup. You can buy it in the West but at quite a high price. Cucumbers, especially if used in summer-glut months, drive down the price with little loss of flavour. If using dried black mushrooms, soak them in hot water for about 30 minutes and then slice. Strain the liquid and add it to the soup.

SERVES 3–4

2 large cucumbers, peeled, deseeded and cut into fingernail-sized cubes
2 dried black mushrooms or 4 fresh mushrooms, sliced
1½ pints (900ml) chicken stock
salt and white pepper (to taste)

a pinch of sugar
8oz (225g) well-flavoured ham (preferably smoked), finely chopped (supermarket off-cuts are perfect)
1 teaspoon *tung choi* or preserved Chinese vegetable (optional)

1. Put the cucumbers and mushrooms into a saucepan, add the stock, seasoning and sugar, and bring to the boil.

2. Cover and simmer for 15 minutes. Stir in the ham, and *tung choi* if using, and simmer for another 5 minutes.

VARIATION
✦ Sometimes it is so satisfying to have a thin soup like this to clear one's palate. But if you find it too bland after the fiery recipes we have given you, sprinkle a chopped chilli and 1 teaspoon toasted sesame seeds over the top before serving.

SPICY CHANNA DHAL SOUP

✦

SRI LANKANS do like their *paripoo* or (lentils)! Besides eating them as a vegetable accompaniment to rice, they are combined with onions and tomatoes to make appetising soups. Sometimes served with the *dhal* soft yet whole, or else cooked until they fall into a thick purée, this soup is very refreshing, thin and spicy, and provides an excellent contrast to richer, creamier dishes. Full of protein, it is very healthy too. The tempered spices are fried in hot oil until they go brown and pop, then added at the end to boost the flavour.

Although this soup is best eaten with rice and curries (but we would say that, wouldn't we?!), it is also delicious served with hunks of warm French bread, Mango Acharu (p.26) and sliced tomatoes drizzled with a little oil, sprinkled with sea salt, fresh black pepper and torn fresh basil leaves. A vegetarian banquet!

SERVES 4–5

2 tablespoons mustard oil or other
    vegetable oil

For the paste
2 cloves garlic, peeled
2 onions, peeled and roughly chopped
a ½ inch (1cm) piece ginger, peeled

For the soup
1 X 14oz (400g) can chopped tomatoes
½ teaspoon ground turmeric
1 teaspoon ground coriander
½ teaspoon ground cumin
4oz (110g) *channa* (chickpeas), soaked in
    water overnight, then rinsed in plenty
    of fresh water, *or* 1 X 14oz (400g) can
    chickpeas

2 dried red chillies, chopped
1 small carrot, peeled and diced
1 stalk celery, diced
1 teaspoon sugar
½ teaspoon ground black pepper

For the tempered spices
1 dessertspoon oil
½ teaspoon black peppercorns, coarsely
    ground
½ teaspoon mustard seeds
2 curry leaves (optional)
1 small onion, peeled and finely sliced

1. To make the paste, liquidise the garlic, onions and ginger with 2 table-spoons water, adding a little extra water if needed. Heat the oil in a heavy-based saucepan, add the paste and fry for 3–4 minutes or until the 'rawness' disappears. Taste a little of the mixture to make sure.

2. Add 1½ pints (900ml) water and all the soup ingredients. Bring to the boil, cover and simmer for 25–30 minutes.

3. To make the tempered spices, heat the oil in a saucepan, add the spices, and fry until they pop. Stand by with a saucepan lid to stop any flying out of the pan – more fun than it sounds! Add the onion and fry until it begins to turn slightly brown. Stir into the hot soup, simmer for a further 5 minutes to allow the flavours to develop, and serve.

PENANG LAKSA

✦

W E ARE always being asked if it is 'safe' eating on the streets. All we can say is that we have rarely suffered in Thailand, Malaysia, Singapore or Sri Lanka from bad tummies. We are careful naturally to eat from traders who look clean, who have tidy stalls and are cooking up fresh supplies regularly but then we are careful where we dine in the West, too. The Malaysian authorities jealously guard their world-famous reputation for cheap, good, clean food. Hawkers in Penang have to be registered and are routinely checked for diseases and sent on courses on safe food-handling. So eat and enjoy!

This recipe is one of our favourites. *Laksa*, a Malaysian national dish, is here given a distinctive fishy twist – worthy of an island paradise. Satisfying, spicy and filling, it is well worth trying.

SERVES 4–5

2 large mackerel, cut into diagonal slices crossways
2 teaspoons salt
½ teaspoon freshly ground black pepper
3 stalks lemon grass, chopped, *or* the grated rind of 2 large lemons
4oz (110g) chopped spring onion
4 chillies
1 teaspoon chopped fresh galangal or ginger
3 stalks Thai basil leaves or fresh ordinary basil
1 tablespoon oil
1 teaspoon sugar
1 teaspoon ground turmeric

½ teaspoon shrimp paste (*trasi* or *blachan*) *or* 1 tablespoon fish sauce *or* 1 teaspoon ground dried shrimp (optional)
1 teaspoon tamarind pulp or lemon juice
1lb (450g) boiled thick rice noodles or egg noodles

For the garnish
1 small cucumber, shredded
½ small lettuce heart, shredded
2 pineapple rings, crushed, *or* 3 tablespoons crushed pineapple, drained of juice
a few fresh mint leaves
2 fresh chillies, chopped
1 small onion, peeled and finely sliced

1. Take the heads off the mackerel and save for stock later. Put the slices of fish in a saucepan with the salt, pepper and 2 pints (1.2 litres) water. Bring to the boil for 10 minutes or until the fish is cooked. Take the fish out of the stock and remove all the bones.

2. Put the fish bones and heads into the fish water and boil for 15 minutes. Strain and reserve the stock.

3. Put the lemon grass or rind, spring onion, chillies, and galangal or ginger in a blender and whizz with enough water to make a paste.

4. Wash out the saucepan, then return the stock and all the remaining ingredients, except the fish, to the pan. Bring to the boil and simmer for 20 minutes.

5. Add the fish, reheat and garnish with all or some of the garnish ingredients before serving.

STUFFED SQUID SOUP

✦

ANOTHER one of our stable of 'clear soup meals', we were hard-pressed to decide whether to include this recipe in soups or seafood; it would sit happily in either. A bowlful of this should be enough to satisfy the hungriest appetite; served with rice, it could also become the centrepiece of a more elaborate meal.

SERVES 4

8oz (225g) minced pork or good-quality pork sausages (remove the skins or your soup will be very rubbery!)

4oz (110g) prawns (preferably cold water prawns) or crab sticks, finely chopped

½ teaspoon soy sauce

¼ teaspoon ground white pepper

11oz (300g) small squid, cleaned and tentacles chopped

2 pints (1.2 litres) chicken stock *or* 3 chicken stock cubes dissolved in the same quantity of water

½ teaspoon *tung choi* or preserved Chinese vegetable (optional)

3 cloves garlic, peeled and crushed

1 teaspoon black peppercorns, coarsely crushed

½ teaspoon sugar

1 teaspoon fish sauce (optional)

1 spring onion, washed, trimmed and chopped

1 tablespoon fresh coriander leaves, chopped (optional)

1. Mix the pork, prawns or crab sticks, soy sauce and white pepper together and use to stuff the squid loosely. Any leftover mixture can be formed into small balls to drop into the soup.

2. Put the chicken stock into a large saucepan with the *tung choi* if using, garlic, black pepper, sugar, and fish sauce if using, and bring to the boil. Add the squid and any meatballs or fishballs. Boil for 10–15 minutes or until the squid is cooked (remove a piece and taste).

3. Add the spring onion, and coriander if using, remove from the heat, and serve.

VARIATION

✦ You can jazz up the finished soup, if you like, with a little chopped chilli and a few drops of soy sauce.

VELVET CRAB AND SWEETCORN SOUP

✦

THIS IS one of the most popular and easily cooked South-East Asian soups. Originating in China, the blend of crab and sweetcorn is very appealing, especially to children, so we make no apologies for including such a well-known dish. With our cheating short cuts, you will never again be caught out by unexpected guests! All you need is a can of creamed sweetcorn and a tin of crabmeat or some crabsticks in the freezer. What could be easier?

SERVES 4–6

1½ pints (900ml) chicken stock *or* 3 chicken stock cubes dissolved in the same quantity of water

10 crab sticks, chopped, or 1 × 8oz (225g) can crab meat

½ teaspoon sugar

1 teaspoon ginger juice (place slices of fresh ginger in a garlic crusher and press firmly until the juice is extracted)

1 × 8oz (225g) can creamed corn

1 teaspoon sherry

1 teaspoon oil (preferably sesame)

1½ teaspoons cornflour mixed with 1 tablespoon water

salt and white pepper (to taste)

1 spring onion, washed, trimmed and chopped

1. Mix all the ingredients together in a saucepan, except the spring onion, and bring to the boil. Taste and adjust the seasoning.

2. Sprinkle the spring onion over the top just before serving.

VARIATION

✦ If you omit the sweetcorn and instead use 2 tablespoons sliced bamboo shoots, 2 tablespoons oil, 1 coarsely grated white radish, and 8oz (225g) shredded spinach, then whisk in 2 beaten egg whites to form thin white threads in the hot soup at the last moment, you have Vietnamese Crab Soup (*Canh Cua*). Garnish with the spring onion and also a little shredded chilli and some fresh coriander leaves.

SPICED CREAMY PUMPKIN SOUP

✦

ONE OF the most tiring things we had to do when growing our small spice business was to attend interminable craft and food shows. It was lovely meeting the public but also very uncomfortable being on show all the time. Inevitably someone would catch us stuffing our faces with something bad, like Chandra's favourite doughnuts or endless rolls or sandwiches. We were always eating – from sheer boredom.

At the last show we went to, we really couldn't face any more bread, fudge or ice-cream (now you know why we are always losing the battle of the bulge!) and then Rani came across hot pumpkin soup. Suitably boosted with dollops of our fiery hot relishes, it was an instant reviver. Here is our adapted recipe – Tiger Lily style. Although it's not strictly street food, the caterers were selling it from a trestle table and we think it is very tasty!

SERVES 4–6

1 tablespoon oil
1 teaspoon mustard seeds
1 × 2lb (900g) pumpkin, peeled, de-seeded and cut into small chunks
1 stalk celery, diced
1 clove garlic, peeled and crushed
1 large onion, peeled and diced
1 small potato, peeled and chopped into chunks
1 teaspoon salt
1 teaspoon freshly ground black pepper
1 teaspoon ground dried prawns (optional)

4oz (110g) coconut cream
1 small chilli, chopped
1 red pepper, cut into small cubes
½ teaspoon ground cumin
1 teaspoon ground coriander
½ teaspoon chilli powder
⎫ or 2 teaspoons good-quality curry powder ⎭
1 teaspoon lemon juice
1–2 tablespoons thick yoghurt (optional)

1. Heat the oil in a large saucepan, fry the mustard seeds until they 'pop', then add 2 pints (1.2 litres) water and all the remaining ingredients, except the lemon juice and yoghurt, and bring to the boil.

2. Simmer for 30 minutes or until the vegetables are cooked. Stir in the lemon juice and mash with a potato masher until it is the consistency you like (from smooth as a baby's proverbial to as rough as Clint Eastwood's chin!). Taste and adjust the seasoning, and if liked stir in some thick yoghurt to make it even creamier.

Breads

W E HAVE stressed time and time again our great devotion to rice but there are those in our family who would trade a bowl of rice any day for a serving of light, flaky *rotis* or parathas.

Mum was brought up in Northern China where the arid soil and the cold climate were more suitable for raising wheat than rice. She loves noodles, dumplings, buns and pancakes, especially nowadays, as she says the grains of rice irritate her gums when they get under her dentures. This ensures that at any family dinner she is specially catered for and only fed the dishes she enjoys most!

John, Chandra's husband, was equally crafty growing up in Guyana, South America. He was so thin and wiry he was known as 'wire man' (as in coat hanger) and exceptionally fussy about his food, absolutely refusing to eat rice in any form. Every day his long-suffering mother would be forced to cook *rotis* just for him (when the rest of the family settled for whatever was on the menu), as she was worried he might otherwise disappear altogether!

A rude awakening was in store when he married Chandra. Blinded by love, he married her before checking to see if she could cook *roti*. At the time, she was hard-pressed to produce a pancake (but able to cook perfect rice), and thus managed what his mother had never been able to do – make him eat and appreciate rice. When the alternative was starvation, this was not so difficult! Since then Chandra has managed to master the intricacies of making *roti* which she now cooks for him as a special treat, reward or bribe . . .

In Kuala Lumpur, Malaysia, we loved watching the *roti canai* makers at work. Rolling out the paper-thin dough, they would swing a small lump of it above their heads until daylight could be seen through the gossamer-fine circles. They would then slap it on a *tawa* (hotplate), brush ghee over it and fold it with a flourish into a multi-layered gastronomic treat. (Neisha, Chandra's daughter, once tried to duplicate this seemingly easy action. Grabbing a lump of dough, she swung it with abandon, whereupon it shot across the room and splattered against the wall like some abstract work of art! We would recommend that you roll the dough – less fun but more accurate.)

ROTI CANAI

✦

R OTI is the generic term for unleavened Indian bread and *roti canai* is the very light, flaky bread found in Malaysia and other South-East Asian countries, where the dough is lovingly brushed with melted butter or ghee before being cooked.

Serve these *rotis* with a selection of curries, or as a snack with butter and jaggery (palm sugar).

They can be frozen if they are tightly wrapped in foil. Reheat them gently under the grill for a few minutes. Do not overheat or they will become hard and brittle.

SERVES 4–6

9oz (250g) plain flour	3fl oz (75ml) warm milk or water
½ teaspoon salt	5oz (150g) butter or ghee, melted
½ teaspoon sugar	1 medium egg, beaten

1. Sift the flour, salt and sugar together into a large bowl.

2. Add the milk or water, melted butter or ghee and the beaten egg and mix into a soft dough. Add more water or milk if required.

3. Knead for 5 minutes, wrap in cling film and leave to rest for approximately 2–3 hours (or overnight).

4. Divide the dough into 8–12 balls.

5. Shape each ball into a thin circle and brush each one with ½ teaspoon ghee or melted butter. Roll each circle into a tight cigar-like shape, coil it round in a cone-shaped spiral, then push the centre down to make a small flat mound. (See illustrations opposite).

6. Repeat step 5 twice more. (This will give you the flaky layers when the *roti* is cooked.)

7. Roll each *roti* out lightly for the last time (to keep the air inside) and

cook over a moderate heat in a heavy-based frying pan, brushing both sides with ghee or melted butter, until golden brown.

STEP 5

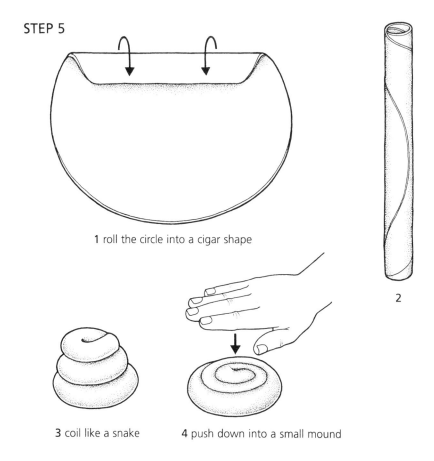

1 roll the circle into a cigar shape

2

3 coil like a snake   4 push down into a small mound

VARIATION

◆ Try *roti canai* stuffed with egg, one of Rani's favourite dishes. Make a spicy omelette by frying 1 chopped onion with 1 clove crushed garlic in 1 tablespoon ghee or vegetable oil until brown. Add 1 finely sliced green chilli, ½ teaspoon each ground coriander and ground cumin, and ¼ teaspoon ground turmeric. Fry gently for approximately 1 minute. Add 4 beaten eggs and ½ teaspoon salt, and cook both sides until set. When cooked, divide the omelette into squares (the same number of portions as the *roti canai* you are making). Make the *roti* to step 7, rolling it as thinly as possible. Place the dough on the pan and put the filling in the middle, drawing the edges of the dough over it to make a neat parcel. Spread lightly with ghee or melted butter and cook both sides until crispy and golden in colour.

PURIS (BAKES)

✦

WHEN WE started our company, Tiger Lily, we did some market research for our products at a local car boot sale in North London. We made some *puris* for our lunch, stuffed with vegetable curry, and had so many envious remarks from the 'punters' that we made a few more the following Saturday and sold them along with our relishes. The *puris* (known as 'bakes' in the West Indies) were so popular that we would regularly get a queue of patient people, salivating while they waited and looking anxious in case we sold out before it was their turn to be served.

These breads are extremely quick and easy to make. When deep-fried in hot oil, they puff out, forming a pocket in the middle which is tailor-made for tasty fillings. It is important to ensure that the oil is smoking hot before cooking them. This way, they cook so fast that they hardly absorb any oil. They are delicious just as they are, with curries or stews. If you want to fill them, make sure the fillings are on the dry side as too much gravy will make them soggy.

Puris can be made in advance and freeze very well, wrapped tightly in foil, although they will not remain puffy. To reheat, place the foil package in a slow oven, at 150°C/300°F/Gas Mark 2, for approximately 10 minutes.

SERVES 4–6

4oz (110g) self-raising flour
½ teaspoon salt

½ teaspoon sugar
vegetable oil

1. Sift the flour into a bowl with the salt and sugar and add 4fl oz (110ml) water gradually until you have a pliable dough. Add more water if necessary.

2. Knead the dough for about 5 minutes, then leave to rest for about 2 hours, covered with a damp cloth to prevent it getting dry.

3. Knead again, then divide the dough into 12 equal-sized balls.

4. Using plenty of flour, roll each ball into a saucer-sized circle, keeping the rest of the dough covered with the damp cloth.

5. Heat the oil until smoking hot in a wok or deep frying pan. Drop each *puri* into the hot oil and, as it tries to float to the surface, push it down gently or spoon the oil over it. It should puff up in about half a minute, when it should be turned over and cooked for about the same length of

time. (If the *puri* is hard or does not puff up, it is probably because the oil is not hot enough or because you are cooking it too long.)

6. Remove from the pan, drain well on kitchen paper and serve immediately.

VARIATIONS

✦ To make stuffed *puris*, slit a pocket in the puffed-up *puri* and use a filling of your choice. We especially recommend Tiger Lily Lamb Kebabs (p.107), taken off the skewers first, or Goat Curry (p.116).

✦ Make cocktail-sized *puris* and stuff them with a variety of fillings for parties – an exciting change from rolls and *vol au vents*.

PARATHAS

✦

ALTHOUGH forbidden to go fishing after dark by his mother, Chandra's husband John used to spend many balmy star-studded nights far out at sea, in a tiny boat with his neighbour Cyril, casting their nets to catch exotic tropical fish. These would supplement the family diet or be sold in the local market. After each of these excursions, John would be soundly whipped for disobedience, but the following night would find him fishing again, armed with a cushion to protect his tender behind.

The reward for a hard night at sea would be a breakfast of stuffed paratha – a flaky, airy, delicate bread filled with spicy vegetable, meat or chicken curry. Available freshly cooked and piping hot from the many street vendors, this delicacy originated in India, and was transported to the West Indies by the indentured Asian slaves brought to work in Guyana.

The secret of making a good paratha is letting the dough rest before rolling it out, and having the pan smoking hot before cooking it. The technique is easier than it sounds, and, once mastered, dozens of parathas can be made in no time at all.

Cooked, plain parathas freeze very well for up to a month. To reheat, defrost them, then grill individually under a moderate heat for a minute on each side, brushing them with oil or melted butter.

Versions of parathas can be found all over South-East Asia and on almost every Caribbean island. Do try making your own – they are well worth the extra effort!

SERVES 4–6

18oz (500g) self-raising flour
1 teaspoon salt

8fl oz (225ml) vegetable or sunflower oil

1. Sift 14oz (400g) flour, with the salt, into a bowl. Gradually add 2 tablespoons oil and 8fl oz (225ml) water, until the mixture forms a soft dough and comes away cleanly from the sides of the bowl. The water required will depend on the absorbency of the flour used. Turn the dough onto a clean, floured surface and knead well for 5 minutes.

2. Leave to rest in the bowl, covered with a clean, damp tea towel, for a minimum of 30 minutes (longer if possible).

3. Turn the dough onto a clean, floured surface and knead well, then roll it into a rough square, approximately 18 inches (45cm), and liberally anoint the surface with a quarter of the remaining oil before sifting a light covering of flour over it.

4. Lightly oil a flat, heavy-based frying pan, and put it over a medium heat. While the pan is heating, roll the dough up like a swiss roll, and cut into 12 evenly sized slices. With the cut sides uppermost, roll the dough into very thin circles, the size of small dinner plates. Cover with a clean, damp tea towel to keep them moist.

STEP 3   **STEP 4**

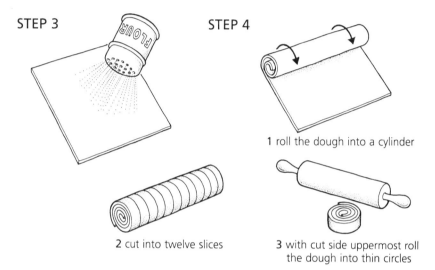

1 roll the dough into a cylinder

2 cut into twelve slices

3 with cut side uppermost roll the dough into thin circles

5. When the pan is smoking hot, slap a paratha onto it and leave until air bubbles start appearing on the surface (approximately 1–2 minutes, depending on the heat of the pan). Brush with oil, turn it over and cook the other side for another 1–2 minutes, moving it around the pan to prevent it burning. Moisten a kitchen towel or cloth with oil and use it to press the edges of the paratha down to ensure they are well cooked.

6. Remove the paratha from the pan, clap it a couple of times between your hands, which will make it break slightly and become very flaky, then fold into quarters and wrap tightly in foil to keep warm. They will be very hot, so be careful. Repeat until all the parathas are cooked.

VARIATIONS

◆ Remove the cooked parathas from the foil, open them out flat and fill with a spicy stuffing of your choice. Fold up like an envelope, tucking in the corners so the stuffing does not fall out. Serve immediately and take a well-earned bow!

◆ Spread with butter and jam for an exotic change from toast at breakfast.

DHALPURIS
Parathas Stuffed with Lentils

✦

A DHALPURI is a paratha, stuffed with a spicy lentil filling, which provides an excellent, protein-packed and tasty accompaniment to curries or an ideal party or picnic dish. The filling should be floury rather than pasty, so make sure that you drain and dry the lentils properly, after they have been parboiled.

SERVES 4–6

1 quantity Parathas (p.46)

For the filling
1lb (450g) dried split peas
salt

5 cloves garlic, peeled and crushed
1 small onion, peeled and chopped
1 green chilli
½ teaspoon ground black pepper
1 teaspoon ground cumin

1. First make the filling. Parboil the split peas in double their own volume of water (to which has been added 1 tablespoon salt), for 10–12 minutes, until they are partially cooked.

2. Drain the peas thoroughly, and dry well on kitchen paper. Add ½ teaspoon salt and the other ingredients and grind in a mortar and pestle or a food processor until you have a fine powdery texture. Taste and add more seasoning if required. Set aside while you make the dough for the parathas.

3. Make the parathas according to the recipe, up to and including step 4.

4. Spread about 2 tablespoons filling in the middle of each circle and form the dough into a ball with your hands, making sure the filling is totally enclosed by the dough.

5. Roll out gently into very thin circles on a floured surface, and cook individually on the smoking hot pan, brushing both sides with oil, until lightly brown on both sides. This should take about a minute on each side.

6. Wrap the cooked parathas in a clean tea towel or a piece of foil to keep warm.

ORIENTAL PANCAKES

✦

THAI and Vietnamese cooks love pretty presentation and this includes the almost fanatical wrapping of food into dainty little parcels which are then dipped into spicy sauces and eaten. The wrappers can be made of all sorts of ingredients – simple omelettes, very thin pancakes made of wheat or rice flour, leaves of lettuce or wilted spinach.

Sometimes they excel themselves and use two or more wrappers. For example, small bowls of spiced meat, shredded cucumber and spring onion (similar, in fact, to the Chinese ingredients in Peking Duck), pancakes and lettuce are placed in front of guests. Each person spoons a small portion of filling into the centre of a pancake, rolls this into a small cylinder, wraps it in a lettuce leaf, then dips the whole exquisite roll into a selection of sauces and eats. Mmmm!

Normally these pancakes are eaten cold – they will stay pliable and soft. If you must, you can reheat them by steaming for a few minutes but it is not necessary. Leftover pancakes freeze successfully. Put a layer of greaseproof paper in between each pancake, then wrap in cling film. Defrost only as many as you will need for each meal.

Serve them with Easy Honey-Spiced Roast Duck (p.85), or try shredding and putting the following into bowls: 1lb (450g) Honey-Roasted Pork (p.115); ½ cucumber; 6 spring onions; 4 stalks celery; 4 red chillies; a handful of chopped roasted and salted peanuts; a handful of chopped fresh coriander. Serve with a selection of chilli sauces and bowls of soy and fish sauce.

MAKES 30–50 depending on size; allow at least 5 each – they go fast!

1lb (450g) plain flour	9 fl oz (250ml) boiling water
1 teaspoon salt	extra flour
1 tablespoon vegetable oil	

1. Sift the flour and salt into a bowl, then add the oil.

2. Pour in enough of the water to mix into a soft dough. Knead for a few moments, then cover with a cloth to keep warm.

3. Break off small balls and roll out on a floured surface until almost transparent.

4. Heat a non-stick frying pan, and dry-fry the pancakes for a minute or so on each side.

Rice

'RICE IS NICE'. If we could, we would have this simple mantra tattooed on to our foreheads. How we love it – in all its incarnations, from pure and simple white and single-grained, through the aromatic slim-lined Basmati of India, through the fragrant Thai rounded grains and sticky glutinous starch, to the red and brown unpolished grains of country rices.

More people eat rice than any other grain or vegetable on this good earth and they have found ways of making it enticing and palatable. For many countries it is not only the basis of the staple diet but also a valuable cash crop, bringing in much-needed revenue. And so it is doubly revered.

In the Orient, rice is usually cooked in the morning and stored, covered, in a cool place. Family members can then 'graze' whenever the mood takes them, eating a bowlful with a spicy sauce or sambol or a simple accompaniment such as fried sprats. The rice would never be heated up – why waste valuable fuel? Mother used to make us a bowl of rice, hot water and ordinary boiled peanuts (not the salted, roasted type but fresh ones from a healthfood store). It sounds ghastly but it is very tasty.

In Indonesia, a special party dish is *Nasi Kuning* (Yellow Rice) which is tinted with turmeric and heaped into a cone, said to represent the mythical Hindu mountain of Meru. Yellow is the colour of royalty in this country, and one of the four sacred colours for Balinese Hindus who celebrate the rituals of planting and reaping in their religious ceremonies.

Eaten with savouries, sweetened as a pudding, milled and turned into flour and from thence to pastries and even made into noodles – yes, rice is *very* nice!

OPPOSITE *Top to bottom:* Spiced Creamy Pumpkin Soup (page 40) and Coconut and Galangal Soup (page 32)

NASI KUNING
Indonesian Yellow Rice

✦

VERY similar to Sri Lankan yellow rice, only spicier, this dish is served at festivals, garnished with sliced hard-boiled egg, cucumber, fried prawns and thin slivers of red and green chilli. It looks spectacular as a centrepiece served with a variety of curries.

SERVES 6–8

1lb (450g) long-grain rice
2 tablespoons oil
1 small onion, peeled and chopped
7oz (200g) creamed coconut dissolved in
    26fl oz (725ml) water
1 stalk lemon grass, chopped
1½ teaspoons salt

1 teaspoon ground turmeric
1 teaspoon ground dried prawns
2–3 curry leaves (optional)
a 1 inch (2.5cm) piece of *rampe* or pandanus leaf (optional)
3 whole black peppercorns, crushed

1. Wash the rice until the water runs clear, showing that all the starch has gone. This stops the grains sticking together.

2. Heat the oil in a heavy-based saucepan, and fry the onion until soft. Add the rice and stir until each grain is coated.

3. Add all the rest of the ingredients, and bring to the boil. Cover with a tight-fitting lid and simmer over a very gentle heat until the rice is cooked. This should take 15–20 minutes.

4. Fluff up with a fork and serve on a large platter with the garnish described above and a selection of curries.

OPPOSITE *Clockwise from top:* Nasi Goreng (page 53), extra Fried Onion Flakes (page 10) and Hot Thai-style Spicy Scallops (page 101)

NASI LEMAK
Coconut Rice

✦

THIS IS found throughout Malaysia, Indonesia, Singapore and, in its fancier guise, as Sri Lanka's premier celebratory rice dish, Milk Rice or *Kiri Bath*. In those jungles where rubber tappers have not been replaced by machines, *Nasi Lemak* is still eaten by hungry workers with the addition of hard-boiled eggs, salted fish, spiced dried prawns, wedges of cucumber, and, of course, lashings of chilli sauce. It is good served with curries, to make a change from plain boiled rice.

SERVES 4

8oz (225g) long-grain rice
1 pint (570ml) canned coconut milk
2 teaspoons salt

2 stalks lemon grass, bashed with a heavy knife, *or* the grated rind of 2 lemons
1 tablespoon desiccated coconut, toasted

1. Wash the rice in plenty of running water. Place in a saucepan with all the ingredients except the toasted coconut.

2. Add 1 pint (570ml) water – enough to reach about 1 inch (2.5cm) above the rice. Bring to the boil, stir well, then tightly cover, turn the heat down and simmer for 15 minutes or until all the liquid is absorbed.

3. Remove the lemon grass if using, place the rice in a serving dish and sprinkle with the toasted coconut.

NASI GORENG
Indonesian Fried Rice

✦

ONE OF Indonesia's best-known dishes, *Nasi Goreng* is found in many South-East Asian countries, with only slight variations in the ingredients used. The usual accompaniments are a fried egg, spicy fried chicken, satay and prawn crackers, balanced with some fresh vegetable salads and various sambols. This is an excellent way to use up leftover rice.

SERVES 4–5

1lb (450g) cooked boiled rice, cold
2 tablespoons oil
2 eggs, lightly beaten
6 spring onions, washed, trimmed and chopped
2 cloves garlic, peeled and crushed, or 2 teaspoons garlic powder
2 red chillies, sliced
1 teaspoon *blachan* or dried shrimp paste (optional)

4oz (110g) mixed cooked meat, chicken or prawns, chopped, or a mixture of any of these
½ teaspoon salt
a pinch of ground turmeric
1 teaspoon tomato purée
1 tablespoon soy sauce
1 cucumber, sliced
4–5 tomatoes, sliced
1 quantity Fried Onion Flakes (p.10)

1. Make sure the rice is absolutely cold or it will absorb the oil and become pasty. Keep it in the fridge overnight to ensure it has dried out. Break up the rice with a fork so that each grain is separate.

2. Use 1 teaspoon of the oil to make very thin omelettes with the beaten eggs. Roll up and cut into thin slivers. Keep to one side.

3. Heat the remaining oil in a wok and stir-fry the spring onions, garlic, chillies, *blachan* or shrimp paste if using, and meat, chicken or prawns. Add the rice and stir-fry on high until everything is combined and the rice is hot. Add the salt, turmeric, tomato paste and soy sauce to taste.

4. Garnish with the slivers of omelette, sliced cucumber, tomatoes and fried onion flakes, and serve.

PINEAPPLE CHICKEN RICE

✦

WE TRAVEL to Northern Sumatra, Indonesia, for this all-in-one meal which is ideal when entertaining or for a family lunch or supper. Although the cashew nuts are optional they do add a delicious bite. This dish is on the dry side so, if you do decide to serve it with a curry, select one with plenty of gravy.

SERVES 4–5

2 tablespoons ghee or oil
4 cloves garlic, peeled and crushed
2 bunches spring onions, washed,
 trimmed and chopped
1 stalk lemon grass, bruised
1 red chilli, chopped
a 1 inch (2.5cm) piece ginger, peeled and
 finely chopped
1 teaspoon ground coriander
1 teaspoon ground pepper
½ teaspoon ground cumin
¼ teaspoon grated nutmeg
a 3 inch (8cm) cinnamon stick

4 cardamom pods, bruised
3 cloves
1lb (450g) boneless chicken, cut into
 ½ inch (1cm) cubes
1 pint (570ml) chicken stock *or* 1½
 chicken stock cubes dissolved in the
 same quantity of water
1 teaspoon salt
4oz (110g) long-grain rice, washed in
 plenty of running water
4oz (110g) fresh cashew nuts (optional)
1 X 14oz (400g) can pineapple chunks,
 drained

1. Heat the ghee or oil in a large saucepan and stir-fry the garlic and spring onions and all the spices for 3 minutes. Add the chicken and continue stir-frying for a further 3 minutes.

2. Add the chicken stock and salt and cook over a low heat until the chicken is tender. Pick out the chicken pieces and keep to one side. Strain the stock, pushing as much as possible through the sieve. Reserve the stock and rinse out the saucepan.

3. Put the rice (and cashew nuts if using) into the saucepan, add 1 pint (570ml) strained stock and bring to the boil. Cover the pan and simmer for 10 minutes until the rice is nearly cooked. Stir in the diced chicken and the pineapple chunks and continue simmering until all the liquid has been absorbed.

KICHIRI

✦

A LTHOUGH strictly an Indian dish, this is a family favourite. Using equal quantities of lentils and rice, it is both delicious and nourishing, packed with protein. An increasing number of our friends are becoming vegetarians and vegans and this is an ideal way to ensure they are not left out when we entertain. It tastes equally good made with ghee or oil.

SERVES 4–5

4oz (110g) Basmati rice	1 teaspoon ground cumin
4oz (110g) red lentils	1 teaspoon ground coriander
3 tablespoons ghee or vegetable oil	2 cloves
1 large onion, peeled and finely sliced	½ teaspoon mustard seed
2 teaspoons salt	4 curry leaves (optional)
½ teaspoon freshly ground black pepper	
½ teaspoon ground turmeric	

or 2½ teaspoons garam masala

1. Wash the rice and the lentils in plenty of running water and leave to soak for 2 hours. (If you haven't got time to wait, you can leave out this soaking stage and increase the total cooking time by 10 minutes.) Drain well in a colander.

2. Heat the ghee or oil in a large pan and fry the onion until it starts caramelising (turning a lovely golden brown and smelling delicious). Keep half the onion to one side until later.

3. Add the rice and lentils to the remaining onion and stir-fry for 3 minutes until everything is coated with the wonderfully buttery/oily/oniony mixture. Add 1¾ pints (1 litre) water and the rest of the ingredients (except the reserved onion), and bring to the boil. Cover and simmer over a low heat for 15 minutes or until cooked. Do not peek or you will let out essential steam.

4. Fork in the reserved onion and serve.

VARIATION

✦ One very ripe chopped tomato and a pinch of grated nutmeg added at the same time as the rice and lentils make this dish even better. We also sometimes stir in a handful of cooked peas.

VEGETABLE BIRIYANI

✦

I N OUR last book, *Tiger Lily – Flavours of the Orient*, we gave you our dad's recipe for Meat Biriyani which went down a storm. However, we have had letters from people asking if we can include a vegetarian alternative in our next book. We do like this one, so here it is. Happy now?!

SERVES 3–4

4oz (110g) long-grain rice, washed in plenty of running water
1 teaspoon salt
1 teaspoon ground cumin
½ teaspoon coarsely ground black pepper
8oz (225g) onions, peeled and finely sliced
2 tablespoons ghee or oil

8oz (225g) aubergines, chopped into ½ inch (1cm) cubes
½ teaspoon ground turmeric
4oz (110g) green pepper, de-seeded and chopped
8oz (225g) ripe tomatoes, chopped
1 stalk celery, chopped
10fl oz (275ml) yoghurt (optional)

1. Put the rice, 8fl oz (225ml) water, salt, cumin and pepper in a saucepan and bring to the boil. Stir, cover tightly and simmer for 12 minutes until cooked.

2. Fry the onions in a tablespoon of ghee or oil until golden brown. Keep to one side.

3. Mix the aubergines and turmeric together, then fry in the remaining tablespoon of ghee or oil until brown.

4. Layer the ingredients in a large casserole dish, except the reserved onions, starting and ending with the rice. Pour the yoghurt over (if using), cover and bake for 30 minutes at 170°C/325°F/Gas Mark 3.

5. Serve with the reserved onion sprinkled over the top.

VARIATION

✦ As with all our recipes, experiment. Add your favourite vegetables or (sorry veggies!) even cold meat. Just keep roughly to the same weight of ingredients.

Noodles

MANY forms of noodles are found in our homelands. Besides the familiar piles of yellow egg noodles, there are white noodles made of rice flour. These can range from thread-like vermicelli or *meehoon*, through normal-sized noodles, to the inches-broad *kway teow* which are excellent for soaking up sauce.

Egg noodles (made of wheat flour) are called *mee*. In Chinese supermarkets you will see huge glistening piles of them coiled up in individual portions in the chill counter section. They should be used within two days of purchase. Dried egg noodles are available everywhere, an essential item for the store-cupboard. Nothing could be quicker than whizzing up a stir-fry, popping in a packet of cooked noodles, and – hey presto – an appetising meal for four.

There are different forms of rice noodles too. *Kway teow* is available fresh from some Oriental grocers, sometimes flavoured with tiny pieces of dried prawn, chillies or spring onions. They may come folded like army bandages. Panic not! Just use a sharp knife to cut to the size you think you can manage without disgracing yourself by dripping noodles and sauce down your front.

The most familiar rice noodles are sold in large packets like giant Shredded Wheat, tied with ribbon. They are our favourites. (We are rice babies and always choose rice above any other staple.) Known as *meehoon* or rice sticks, they are so easy to use. Simply select the amount you need (be warned, the pesky stuff flies everywhere), soak in hot water for about 15 minutes (or longer in cold) and drain (by which time it will have gone soft and malleable). Then mix with a soup or stir-fry for a substantial one-dish meal.

'Bean thread', 'silver rain', 'cellophane' – there are many lovely names for vermicelli, that amazing, slippery and very nutritious noodle made of mung beans. Chinese, Vietnamese, Thais, Indonesians and Malaysians are all very fond of vermicelli and use it in different ways – to add an unusual texture to soups and spring rolls or to stuff things like chicken wings or squid. Soak transparent vermicelli in boiling water for only 3 minutes before using.

KWAY TEOW
Fried Flat Rice Noodles
✦

YOUNG Johnny, Chandra's 23-year-old son, has long held an unenviable reputation as the 'heathen' of the family for his great love of fast food. Left to his devices, he could quite happily live on pizzas and doner kebabs! In the past, his only claim to culinary expertise, to our knowledge, has been producing lovely cup cakes with a buttercream filling from a packet mix, and customising Pot Noodles to his taste by adding a selection of toppings.

One dark, wintry evening, Chandra was delayed at work and called home to let the family know. When she finally reached the house, tired and irritable at the prospect of cooking dinner, she was greeted by a tremendous clattering of utensils and a most appetising aroma from the kitchen. To her amazement, there was Johnny, wielding chopsticks and a wok with great authority, issuing orders to his sister Neisha (his *sous chef*) on the spices he required, while he effortlessly whipped up a scrumptious dinner for the family.

The resulting masterpiece was a spicy noodle concoction, topped with seafood, chicken and vegetables, resembling the fried *kway teow* (flat rice noodles) which are served on every street corner of Malaysia. This is the recipe from the fast food junkie who, by his own admission, successfully hid the fact that he could cook for well over a decade!

SERVES 4–5

6oz (175g) raw chicken or beef
½ teaspoon salt
½ teaspoon sugar
½ teaspoon sesame oil
½ teaspoon sherry (optional)
1 teaspoon ground black pepper
5oz (150g) mixed green vegetables
  (cabbage, chives, etc)
1 green chilli, roughly chopped
4 cloves garlic, peeled and roughly
  chopped

1 large onion, peeled and roughly
  chopped
2½ tablespoons oil
18oz (500g) mixed seafood (cockles,
  squid, prawns, etc)
10oz (275g) beansprouts
2 tablespoons soy sauce
20oz (575g) fresh rice noodles
2 spring onions, washed, trimmed and
  chopped
1–2 fresh red chillies, finely chopped

1. Slice the chicken or beef into strips and marinate for 15 minutes with the salt, sugar, sesame oil, sherry (if using) and black pepper.

2. Wash and slice the green vegetables into thin matchsticks.

3. Grind the green chilli, garlic and onion into a paste using a mortar and pestle or a food processor. Heat the oil and fry the paste over a medium heat until lightly brown.

4. Add the chicken or beef strips and fry for about 3 minutes until cooked. Add the seafood and fry for a further 2 minutes.

5. Increase the heat, add the green vegetables, beansprouts, soy sauce and 3fl oz (75ml) water and stir-fry for another 2 minutes before adding the noodles.

6. Mix everything very well over the heat for approximately 3 minutes until all the ingredients are cooked, and serve garnished with the spring onions and finely chopped red chillies.

VARIATION

✦ Dried egg noodles may be substituted for the rice noodles if preferred, but need to be cooked according to the instructions on the packet before using in place of the *kway teow*.

SOUP NOODLES WITH PORK RIBS AND TURKEY

◆

THIS famous dish is a Penang hawkers' favourite. We have used turkey instead of the more popular duck because it is so much easier to prepare. Instant stock cubes replace the bubbling cauldrons of duck, chicken and pork bones which are always simmering by the roadside ready to add their flavour to rice and noodles.

SERVES 6

1lb (450g) pork ribs
3 chicken stock cubes
2 teaspoons *tung choi* or preserved Chinese vegetable (optional)
8oz (225g) turkey pieces
1 teaspoon sugar
salt
½ teaspoon ground white pepper
3 cloves garlic, peeled and crushed
2 tablespoons oil
2 fresh green chillies, finely sliced
3 tablespoons soy sauce

1½lb (675g) flat rice noodles or egg noodles
1 small head iceberg or cos lettuce, finely shredded

For the fish balls (optional)
8oz (225g) frozen fish fillets, defrosted
¼ teaspoon salt
¼ teaspoon sugar
½ clove garlic, peeled and crushed
a little egg white (less than ½)

1. If making the fish balls, put all the ingredients in a food processor and whizz until they form a paste. Wet your hands and form the mixture into small balls. Refrigerate until ready to cook.

2. Put the pork ribs, stock cubes, 2½ pints (1.5 litres) water, and the *tung choi* if using, in a saucepan. Bring to the boil, skim, then lower the heat and simmer for about 30 minutes or until the pork is almost tender. Add the turkey pieces, sugar, salt to taste and pepper, and simmer for 10 minutes. Add the fish balls if using, and boil for a further 5 minutes or until they rise to the surface of the soup.

3. Fry the crushed garlic in the oil until fragrant. Keep to one side. Mix the chillies with the soy sauce in a small bowl and put that to one side also.

4. Cook the noodles in boiling salted water according to the instructions on the packet. Mix the noodles with the soup, garnish with the shredded lettuce, pour over the garlic oil and serve, accompanied by the chillies in soy sauce.

HOKKIEN MEE

✦

THIS DISH mixes equal quantities of rice vermicelli with yellow egg noodles and beansprouts in a hot spicy sauce, with pork ribs and prawns. In Malaysia, three times the amount of chilli given here would be used. As we did not think you wanted your tonsils removed, we have toned it down for you! Hokkien traders would not use the pork for Muslim Malays, but add more prawns instead.

If you have some Fried Onion Flakes (p.10) they make an excellent garnish, sprinkled over the top.

SERVES 6

For the soup
2 tablespoons oil
1 tablespoon crushed dried chillies
8oz (225g) pork ribs, cut into small pieces
8oz (225g) prawns (fresh if possible or else the large shell-on pink ones), shelled
1 teaspoon salt
1 teaspoon sugar

For the noodles
8oz (225g) rice vermicelli
8oz (225g) egg noodles
8oz (225g) beansprouts
4oz (110g) spinach, cut into pieces

1. To make the soup, heat the oil and fry the chillies slowly until fragrant. Remove half to serve on top of the noodles. Put the rest of the chillies in a saucepan with 2½ pints (1.5 litres) water and the pork ribs, and simmer for 30 minutes or until the ribs are tender. Add the peeled prawns, salt and sugar, and simmer until the prawns are cooked if raw, or gently reheat for a short time if using cooked prawns.

2. Blanch the rice vermicelli and egg noodles in boiling water for 5 minutes and drain well. Blanch the beansprouts and spinach in boiling water for 2 minutes and drain well.

3. Mix the noodles, beansprouts and spinach together in a large bowl. Pour over the hot soup, arrange the ribs and prawns on top, and pour over the reserved chillies in hot oil.

SEAFOOD MEEHOON

✦

*M*EEHOON is very popular in South-East Asia and variations of this dish are found in nearly every country. Very quick to prepare, *meehoon* is a substantial all-in-one meal. The beauty of it is that you can use any ingredients you may have lurking in the fridge as long as they are still fresh. Most combinations of meat, fish and vegetables are suitable (except for potatoes and aubergines).

SERVES 6–8

8oz (225g) rice vermicelli

8oz (225g) large fresh prawns or large pink ones in their shells

8oz (225g) squid

1 medium courgette, washed and trimmed

2 stalks celery, washed and trimmed

1 medium-sized carrot, peeled

1 medium-sized red or yellow pepper, de-seeded and washed

3 tablespoons oil

1 onion, peeled and finely sliced

1 clove garlic, peeled and crushed

a 1 inch (2.5cm) piece ginger, peeled and crushed

1 fresh chilli, finely chopped

3 eggs

1 teaspoon salt

½ teaspoon ground white pepper

1 tablespoon soy sauce

½ vegetable or chicken stock cube dissolved in 6 tablespoons hot water

1 tablespoon sherry

1. Soak the vermicelli in hot water for 15 minutes, then drain and put to one side.

2. Shell and devein the prawns, clean the squid and cut into rings, saving the tentacles (or buy a bag of frozen squid rings instead).

3. Cut the courgette, celery, carrot and red or yellow pepper into very thin matchsticks about 2 inches (5cm) in length.

4. Heat 2 tablespoons oil in a wok, and fry the onion, garlic and ginger until the onion begins to brown. Add the chilli and vegetables, then the prawns and squid. Fry for about 4 minutes until the seafood is just turning opaque.

5. Beat the eggs, add the salt and make several very thin omelettes using the remaining tablespoon of oil. Roll each omelette and cut into thin strips to decorate the *meehoon*. Keep on one side.

6. Add the pepper, soy sauce, stock and sherry to the *meehoon*, together with the seafood and vegetables, and stir. Adjust the seasoning, adding more salt if required. Turn out onto a large serving dish, and garnish with the omelette strips.

STRINGHOPPER PILAU

✦

A DELICIOUS vegetarian dish beloved of busy Sri Lankan wives with little time to spare.

The Sri Lankan name for stringhoppers is *idi appung*. Over the years the *appung* has been corrupted into the word 'hopper'. And, as this dish closely resembles little lengths of string, it is aptly named indeed.

SERVES 4

8oz (225g) rice vermicelli
2 tablespoons oil
1 onion, peeled and finely sliced
1 large carrot, peeled and grated
4oz (110g) peas
½ green pepper, de-seeded and chopped

1 stalk celery, chopped
2 tablespoons tomato ketchup
1 teaspoon ground turmeric
½ teaspoon chilli powder
1 teaspoon salt

1. Soak the rice vermicelli in plenty of boiling water for 15 minutes, drain and put to one side.

2. Heat the oil in a wok and fry the onion until golden. Add the rest of the vegetables and fry for 3–4 minutes or until the vegetables are just softened.

3. Add the vermicelli, then the tomato ketchup, turmeric, chilli powder, salt and 3 tablespoons water. Stir well to combine, and cook over a low heat until the liquid is absorbed. Taste and adjust the seasoning, and serve.

STEAMED NOODLE PACKETS

✦

AN INTERESTING recipe which comes from Indonesia. There, as in many South-East Asian and Oriental countries, food like this is wrapped in clean banana leaves but we can substitute kitchen foil. Ideal for picnics, these parcels travel well, taste just as scrumptious cold, and make a change from sandwiches.

SERVES 12

1lb (450g) dried egg noodles
1 X 7oz (200g) block coconut cream
6 eggs
1½ teaspoons salt
¼ teaspoon ground white pepper
8oz (225g) minced meat (chicken, turkey, lamb or beef)

4 spring onions, washed, trimmed and chopped
½ teaspoon ground cumin
½ teaspoon lime or lemon juice
1 teaspoon chilli sauce
12 X 12 inch (30cm) squares of foil or banana leaves!

1. Cook the noodles according to the directions on the packet. Drain and put on one side.

2. Mix the coconut cream with 8fl oz (225ml) boiling water. Allow to cool, then add 3 eggs, salt and pepper. Mix the noodles into this mixture.

3. In another bowl mix the other 3 eggs, meat and spring onions, cumin, lime or lemon juice and chilli sauce.

4. Divide the noodle mixture between the 12 squares. Do the same with the meat mixture. Fold each one into a package, securing the edges firmly.

5. Place in a steamer and steam for 45 minutes.

Vegetables

WALKING around Oriental markets is a real feast for the eye. Piles of luscious fruit and vegetables, and mountains of crunchy beansprouts, are carefully laid out on straw mats, ancient balancing scales at the ready, while their owners squat beside them. These street markets are made even more colourful by the many bamboo umbrellas erected over the heads of the sellers, providing welcome shade from the searing heat. In some countries, neat 'lampshade' hats adorn the heads of both men and women.

These vegetables are not like the uniform, sexless objects we see in Western shops. These are glowing with rude health, and they come in all different sizes and shapes. Bulging yellow, purple, orange and green marrows and aubergines; long, thin snake beans; sharp, lime-coloured snap peas as sweet as sugar; leaves of every shape, from thin, pointed water convolvulus (*kang kung*), to heart-shaped spinach, to Oriental cabbage (*bak choi*), to bouquets of needle-sharp chives (*chom sum*) – all are heaped in tantalising piles for the shopper to snap, taste, prod and smell. There's none of this 'Don't touch until it's yours, missus!' for Oriental housewives!

Back in our market place, along with freshly grown produce for sale, there will be gunny (hessian) bags of ground and dried spices, deep red Bombay onions or fat white cloves of garlic strung into ropes, and slabs of tofu floating in huge tubs of water.

Tofu or soya bean curd (made from ground, soaked beans) is now available in Western supermarkets as well as health stores which have stocked it for years. You will usually find it sold in creamy white blocks. More people are gradually becoming accustomed to its bland taste and are starting to discover the many flavours it can take on.

Sometimes tofu can be pressed under a weight to extract most of the liquid, then deep-fried and combined with a spicy mixture of vegetables and sauce. With the general move towards healthy eating, it makes an ideal substitute for meat.

Dried tofu is sold in packets of thin, brittle brown sheets. Cut carefully or broken into 1 inch (2.5cm) squares, it is delicious reconstituted in a sauce. We love it dropped into pork chunks gently stewed in soy sauce, mirin and/or rice wine (or sherry), flavoured with star anise – it adds an interesting chewy texture.

STIR-FRIED TOFU
✦

TOFU IS a vitamin- and protein-packed staple food for the many Buddhists and other vegetarians living in South-East Asia, China and Japan. It is cooked in a number of ways but it is quite delicate so take care, when stir-frying it, not to break it up. Cut the tofu into slices or cubes and very gently stir in at the last possible moment, to soak up the hot, sweet and sour flavours.

This dish is best served with a bowl of freshly boiled white rice.

SERVES 4–6

4oz (110g) broccoli, broken into very small florets

12oz (350g) tofu, drained

3 tablespoons vegetable oil

1 clove garlic, peeled and crushed

a 1 inch (2.5cm) piece ginger, peeled and grated

1 × 8oz (225g) can bamboo shoots, drained and cut into thin strips

1 × 8oz (225g) can water chestnuts, drained and each cut into quarters

4 tablespoons soy sauce

1 tablespoon sweet sherry

1 teaspoon sugar

a pinch of chilli powder

1. Blanch the broccoli by dropping it into a pan of boiling water. Cook for 1–2 minutes or until it turns bright green. Immediately take out and plunge into a bowl of cold water. Drain and keep to one side.

2. If the tofu is not pre-cut, slice it into 1 inch (2.5cm) cubes.

3. Heat the oil in a wok. When smoking, add the garlic and ginger and stir for a few seconds to flavour the oil.

4. Add the tofu and fry until crisp and brown. Remove from the wok, drain on some kitchen paper and keep warm.

5. Put the bamboo shoots, water chestnuts and broccoli in the wok and stir-fry for about 4 minutes.

6. Stir in the soy sauce, sherry, sugar and chilli powder, and then the tofu.

VARIATION

✦ If liked, stir in 1 teaspoon sesame oil with the tofu and sprinkle 1 teaspoon lightly toasted sesame seeds over the dish before serving.

SWEET SOUR CUCUMBER
✦

THIS dish is so simple (requiring no cooking) but is deliciously cool and refreshing, and excellent with grilled or fried fish or barbecued meats.

SERVES 4

2 small to medium-sized cucumbers, washed, peeled and cut into wafer-thin slices
1 tablespoon vinegar
1 teaspoon salt

1–2 teaspoons sugar (to taste)
½ teaspoon freshly ground black pepper
1 teaspoon soy sauce
a dash of sesame oil

1. Mix all the ingredients together and allow to stand for about 1 hour before serving.

VARIATIONS

✦ Add grated carrot or white radish for a change.

✦ Sometimes we add interest by sprinkling over some toasted sesame seeds or mustard seeds ('pop' ½ teaspoon seeds by frying them in a little hot oil first).

CRUNCHY TOFU IN CHILLI LIME SAUCE
✦

A DELICIOUS way to serve tofu – crispy on the outside, meltingly creamy on the inside and enlivened with a tangy, zesty sauce. This is a very tasty alternative to fried fish, chicken or scampi. Garnish with shredded lettuce, cucumber and tomato slices and serve the sauce separately.

SERVES 4

1lb (450g) tofu, drained
4oz (110g) plain flour
1 teaspoon salt and a pinch of ground
    white pepper
a pinch of ground cinnamon
1 egg (medium)
4oz (110g) freshly made breadcrumbs
2 pints (1.2 litres) oil

For the sauce
1 tablespoon arrowroot or cornflour
1 small red chilli, finely chopped
juice and grated rind of 2 limes
1 tablespoon jaggery (palm sugar) or dark
    brown sugar
1 tablespoon fish sauce (optional)
8–10 tablespoons chicken stock or water

1. Slice the tofu, then dust liberally with the flour mixed with the salt, pepper and cinnamon.

2. Beat the egg, and dip the tofu slices in it, then into the breadcrumbs. Place on a plate and refrigerate for half an hour to firm. This helps the breadcrumbs to stick.

3. Mix the arrowroot or cornflour with the chilli, lime juice and rind, sugar, fish sauce if using, and stock or water. Bring to the boil in a small pan until the sauce thickens. If using arrowroot, it will clear. Place in a bowl and keep warm.

4. Bring the oil to a smoking heat in a wok. Add the tofu pieces a few at a time and fry until crisp and golden. Remove with a slotted spoon, drain on kitchen paper and keep warm. Serve immediately.

VARIATION
✦ If you can get them, 1–2 kaffir lime leaves (if using dried ones, soak for a few minutes in boiling water to refresh them), torn into small pieces and added to the sauce before boiling, add to the depth of the lime flavour.

SUPREME MIXED VEGETABLES

✦

WHILE browsing in a bookshop in Kuala Lumpur we came across a delightful book containing a recipe rather like this. Imagine our joy when we went to a nearby restaurant for lunch and saw a similar dish on the menu! Needless to say, we had to do our 'market research' immediately and very delicious it was too.

This dish also looks sensational. The multi-coloured vegetables, served on a bed of plain boiled rice or *Nasi Lemak* (p.52), provide a feast for the eye as well as the palate.

SERVES 4–6

8 baby sweetcorn
8 asparagus tips
4 yellow oyster mushrooms
4oz (110g) tiniest fresh baby mushrooms
  or canned straw mushrooms
1 large carrot, scraped
½ small cucumber
4oz (110g) baby spinach
6–8 tablespoons chicken or vegetable
  stock (use ½ stock cube and water)

salt (to taste)
2 tablespoons cornflour mixed with
  4 tablespoons water
1 teaspoon soy sauce
1 teaspoon rice wine or sherry
1 teaspoon sesame oil
½ teaspoon ground white pepper

1. Wash the baby sweetcorn and cut each one in half. Wash the asparagus tips and cut in half. Rinse the mushrooms with the minimum of water. Cut the carrot and cucumber into thin sticks the length of the other vegetables. Wash the spinach leaves thoroughly.

2. Put the sweetcorn, asparagus and carrot into a pot with the stock, and boil for 4–5 minutes or until almost cooked but still firm. Add the mushrooms, spinach and cucumber and cook for only a few minutes more. Do not overcook.

3. Take out all the vegetables with a slotted spoon and arrange in a pretty pattern on a large flat serving dish, piling the mushrooms in the centre, with the vegetable 'sticks' (including the cucumber) radiating like the spokes of a wheel. Keep warm.

4. Put the salt, cornflour mixture, soy sauce, rice wine or sherry, sesame seed oil and white pepper into the pan with the stock and juices. Bring to the boil and stir until it thickens. Pour the sauce over the vegetables and serve.

CHINESE GREENS

◆

EVER wondered how Chinese restaurants manage to serve such appetising-looking vegetables? The trick is to blanch them in boiling water until they turn the deepest green, remove them immediately and plunge them into a bowl of ice-cold water to stop the cooking process. Keep the vegetables this way until you are ready to stir-fry them quickly, just before serving. Try to use the water they are cooked and soaked in because it contains valuable water-soluble vitamins.

These greens go particularly well with plain boiled white rice and Fried Chicken in Plum Sauce (p.79) or Easy Honey-Spiced Roast Duck (p.85).

SERVES 4–6

1 Chinese cabbage (*bak choi*), weighing about 1½lb (675g)
2 tablespoons oil
½ clove garlic, peeled and crushed
1 slice fresh ginger, peeled and very finely sliced
½ × 14fl oz (400ml) can condensed chicken or mushroom soup
2 tablespoons soy sauce
½ small green chilli, finely sliced
½ teaspoon sugar

1. Wash the cabbage, cut into small squares, then blanch and plunge into cold water as described above.

2. Heat the oil in a wok, fry the garlic and ginger, add the cabbage and stir-fry for 2–3 minutes.

3. Add the rest of the ingredients and bring to the boil. Taste and adjust the seasoning, then serve immediately.

VARIATION

◆ If faced with a glut of lettuces in the summer, try using them in this recipe. It may seem strange, cooking this traditional salad leaf, but do try it – it's very tasty.

THAI RED BEAN CURRY

✦

A REALLY easy, unusual and appetising vegetable curry (unlike some traditional Indian curries which can be heavy and cloying, with too much emphasis on oil and spices). If you have some sauce left over, you can keep it in a sealed container in the fridge for up to two days or freeze it and make another curry when you are feeling really lazy. Simply put the frozen sauce and 8oz (225g) frozen beans into a pan and boil until cooked, stirring occasionally.

This recipe uses green beans – the 'red' in the name refers to the red chillies. If you wish, you can add a touch of paprika to enhance the colour without adding extra heat.

Serve with Thai Duck Curry (p.83) and boiled white rice for a real taste of the Orient.

SERVES 4

1lb (450g) runner beans or French beans, washed and cut into bite-sized pieces
1 teaspoon oil

For the curry sauce
1 tablespoon oil
2 red chillies
1 teaspoon grated ginger
1 clove garlic, peeled

1 stalk lemon grass, chopped, *or*
    1 teaspoon grated lime or lemon rind
2 spring onions, trimmed, washed and roughly chopped
5fl oz (150ml) canned coconut milk
1 teaspoon lemon or lime juice
1 teaspoon fish sauce or 1 teaspoon salt
a pinch of sugar (to taste)

1. Place all the curry sauce ingredients in a blender and liquidise until almost smooth. Keep on one side.

2. Blanch the beans in boiling water, then immediately plunge them into cold water.

3. Heat the oil in a wok, swishing it around the pan. Add the sauce ingredients carefully (it may start to spit and splash).

4. Cook for 10 minutes or until the sauce reduces in bulk and tastes mellow rather than raw.

5. Add the beans, heat through, then taste and adjust the seasoning.

MASAK LEMAK
Malay Cabbage and Potato Curry
✦

A DELICIOUSLY mild, pleasantly spicy, white curry which is so quick and easy to make. It tastes wonderful served with a spicy meat or fish curry, and plenty of rice or *rotis* (p.42).

SERVES 4

1 onion, peeled and finely sliced
2 red chillies, chopped
½ teaspoon *blachan* or dried shrimp paste
  (optional)
1 teaspoon salt

½ teaspoon ground white pepper
1 teaspoon ground turmeric
1 potato, peeled and cut into large chunks
1 small white cabbage, finely shredded
4oz (110g) coconut cream

1. Put all the ingredients, except the cabbage and coconut cream, into a saucepan with 12fl oz (350ml) water, and bring to the boil. Simmer for 10 minutes or until the potato is half-cooked. Add a further 1–2 tablespoons water if the curry gets too dry. Add the cabbage and boil again for 5 minutes.

2. Stir in the coconut cream until it dissolves, check the seasoning and serve at once.

SPICY GREEN LEAF PURÉE

✦

THIS is a vibrantly green, spicy, creamy purée. The texture makes an interesting contrast to the usual crisp, stir-fried and whole vegetable curries of South-East Asia.

A delicious, healthy meal, packed with protein and vitamins, if served with *Dhalpuris* (p.48). The addition of Sri Lankan Fish Curry (p.95) will make it a more substantial meal.

SERVES 4–6

1lb (450g) spinach or other green leafy vegetable
1 medium turnip or ¼ white radish
1 tablespoon butter and 1 teaspoon mustard oil or vegetable oil
½ teaspoon whole brown mustard seeds
½ teaspoon onion seed (optional)
1 medium onion, peeled and finely chopped

1 teaspoon finely grated ginger
1 teaspoon ground turmeric
½ teaspoon chilli powder
1 teaspoon salt
½ teaspoon mixed spice
½ teaspoon ground black pepper
a squeeze of lemon juice (optional)

1. Wash the greens and discard any woody stalks or stems. Shred the leaves and place in a large saucepan. Peel and dice the turnip or radish, and put into the same pan with 2 tablespoons water. Cook over a low heat, uncovered, until the vegetables are tender. Put to one side.

2. Heat the butter and oil and fry the seeds for 1 minute. Add the onion and ginger and fry until the onion is fragrant and golden brown, stirring all the time.

3. Add all the remaining ingredients, except the lemon juice if using, including the cooked vegetables, and cook for 5 minutes or until the liquid evaporates. Taste and add extra seasoning and a squeeze of lemon if liked.

4. Mash or liquidise to a purée and serve warm.

BROCCOLI IN OYSTER SAUCE

✦

BROCCOLI is a superb vegetable. Full of goodness, pretty as a bunch of flowers and with an agreeable crunch (if not over-cooked), it's ideal for stir-fries. Oyster sauce, with its natural affinity to vegetables, complements its flavour perfectly.

SERVES 4

12oz (350g) broccoli, broken into small florets
1 tablespoon vegetable oil
1 clove garlic, peeled and crushed
4 tablespoons oyster sauce

2 teaspoons soy sauce
½ teaspoon ground black pepper
1 teaspoon sesame oil
salt (to taste)

1. Blanch the broccoli in a pan of rapidly boiling water for 1 minute or until it turns bright green. Immediately remove and plunge into a pan of cold water.

2. Heat the oil in a wok and stir-fry the garlic until golden and crispy. Add the broccoli, oyster and soy sauces and black pepper. Stir in the sesame oil, add extra salt if necessary, and serve warm.

VARIATION

✦ If liked, sprinkle the top with 1 tablespoon toasted almond slivers.

BAMBOO SHOOT SALAD

✦

A NORTHERN Thai speciality which is particularly good with roasted chicken or pork.

SERVES 4

1lb (450g) canned bamboo shoots, drained and cut into thin matchsticks

4 spring onions, washed, trimmed and chopped

2 tablespoons sticky rice, dry-fried in a frying pan, then ground in a blender (optional)

2 tablespoons lime juice

½ tablespoon fish sauce

½ small teaspoon dried chillies, crushed

½ teaspoon sugar

1. Simply mix all the ingredients together and serve.

HEALTHY STIR-FRIED VEGETABLES

✦

S TREET food often includes crunchy, fresh stir-fried mixed vegetables and sometimes the best recipes come about through sheer luck. Rani was suffering as a result of eating too much rich food, and so she concocted this dish one day. It must win the prize for the simplest, healthiest, quickest recipe in the book. Do try it – it tastes so good.

SERVES 4

1 medium onion, peeled and very thinly sliced

4oz (110g) button mushrooms, rinsed in water and sliced

4oz (110g) beansprouts, rinsed

4oz (110g) Chinese cabbage (*bak choi*), cut into pieces and rinsed in water

1–2 teaspoons fish sauce

1. Use a heavy-based frying pan or wok. Put all the vegetables in together and stir-fry (no oil needed) for 2 minutes or until the vegetables lose their rawness but not their crunch. The water clinging on to the leaves gives enough liquid for the vegetables to steam.

2. Stir in the fish sauce to taste, and serve.

Poultry

CHICKEN is a very popular food in the East and no wonder. Not very much work is needed to keep a few fowl – you just leave them to scratch in the dust, squawk and lay eggs. Our tender hearts used to be touched when we went to visit relations who lived away from the Sri Lankan capital, Colombo, and its convenience stores with their deep-freezers. We knew that Cook would soon be chasing some unfortunate which would then end up in the pot for our pleasure. These chickens were much smaller than their Western counterparts (due in part, no doubt, to the extra exercise they got, running away from Cookie!). Ours were scrawny, yellow and stringy, and often quite tough – but oh the flavour! Long, slow cooking would tenderise the toughest old boilers, while the younger fowl would be reserved for frying.

Every Oriental market has its live animal section. Here you will find old hens sitting dejectedly in bamboo cages, staring with listless eyes; and young but useless cockerels, still fluttering and trying to make a break for freedom with their scaly feet tied together. These days, we are far too squeamish to buy something that can look at us reproachfully before it's turned into dinner – but most South-East Asian housewives choose their families' meals live and clucking, with nary a qualm, fresh as fresh can be.

SPICY FRIED CHICKEN WINGS

✦

NOT FOR nothing do so many take-aways in the UK offer spicy chicken wings. Madly popular, they seem to walk (or fly) out on their own! In the Orient, chicken wings are much prized. In China, especially, they are almost as popular as chicken feet – which are served deep-fried like peanuts. One eats what little meat there is on the scaly portions, then spits the claws out into the gutter. There are parts of Hong Kong where one walks on a crunchy path of these discarded nails.

In one Chinese supermarket in Soho we noticed the labelling on the frozen claws had gone a bit awry – and the reluctant buyer was exhorted to purchase 'chicken paws'. Before predictably saying 'yuck', consider the Oriental abhorrence of cheese – to them it is like eating hardened rotten milk. Each to his or her own, as they say. Better still, why not try this far more palatable recipe?

Marinating the chicken overnight makes it tender, juicy and full of flavour. Serve as a starter with cucumber batons and a spicy dipping sauce, or with boiled rice or noodles as part of a main meal. This dish can also be made with fillets of white fish.

SERVES 4

1lb (450g) chicken wings
½ teaspoon salt
½ teaspoon sugar
1 teaspoon onion salt
1 teaspoon celery salt
2 teaspoons mixed dried herbs, finely
  crumbled

1–2 teaspoons chilli powder (use the
  larger amount if you like very hot food)
1 tablespoon vinegar
4oz (110g) self-raising white flour
2 pints (1.2 litres) oil

1. Cut each wing into 3 pieces. Use the wing tips for soup or discard.

2. Put the chicken wings in a bowl and mix with all the ingredients except the flour and oil. Leave to marinate in the fridge overnight.

3. The next day, put the flour in a paper or plastic bag, add the wings, a few at a time, and shake until they are thickly coated.

4. Heat the oil in a wok until smoking. Lower the heat and fry the wings in batches, turning occasionally until crisp, golden and cooked through.

ROAST LIME AND GINGER CHICKEN

✦

EVERY time we sit at the table and tuck into a chicken meal we should say a big thank you to the South-East Asian jungle fowl, the grandfather and grandmother of all our domestic fowl.

Chickens back home are very similar to their wild cousins. The cock's plumage is wonderfully colourful, with long, trailing tail feathers, and he preens and struts around most compounds with supreme arrogance. The meat is tough and yellow in colour but so full of flavour. It makes a wonderful curry.

This recipe is found in South-East Asia and also the Caribbean – slavers introduced it, and the humble fowl, on their travels. Chicken prepared this way is equally delicious split in half and barbecued instead. Street traders sometimes cut it into quarters as well before barbecuing it, or they leave it whole and chop it into bite-sized pieces after it's cooked.

SERVES 4

2 tablespoons grated fresh ginger
2 cloves garlic, peeled and crushed
1 small onion, peeled and finely chopped
1 teaspoon salt
1 teaspoon coarsely ground black pepper
1 stalk lemon grass, crushed
1 × 4–5lb (1.8–2.2kg) roasting chicken

2 tablespoons coconut oil or melted butter
3 tablespoons lime juice
2 tablespoons lime or orange marmalade
1 teaspoon cornflour mixed with 1 tablespoon water

1. Using a blender or food processor, make a paste with the ginger, garlic, onion, salt, pepper and lemon grass. Rub the chicken well, both inside and out, then leave to let the flavours sink in, either overnight or for at least 2 hours, in a refrigerator.

2. Set the oven to 180°C/350°F/Gas Mark 4. Heat the coconut oil or melted butter, lime juice and marmalade in a small saucepan, and pour over the chicken.

3. Put the chicken on a trivet over a tray of water (to catch the drips) and roast for 1–1½ hours or until the chicken is golden brown.

4. Reduce the water in the tray, if necessary, by boiling in a small saucepan, add the cornflour mixture, and boil until it thickens. Serve with the chicken.

FRIED CHICKEN IN PLUM SAUCE

✦

THIS recipe is made for sticky fingers, lots of paper towels and inelegant eating – but my, isn't it wonderful!

Our first choice of an accompaniment would be rice, and more rice – of course! But, as this dish is especially good for party buffets, crispy French bread and a green salad or coleslaw would be equally good (well, almost as good!).

SERVES 4–5

1 X 2lb (900g) chicken
1½ teaspoons five spice powder
2 slices ginger, peeled and grated
2 tablespoons soy sauce
4 tablespoons self-raising flour
2 tablespoons cornflour

2 pints (1.2 litres) oil
4oz (110g) plum or hoisin sauce
½ teaspoon vinegar
1 teaspoon soy sauce
salt (to taste)
1½ tablespoons toasted sesame seeds

1. Cut the chicken into 16 pieces and remove the skin. Mix the chicken pieces with the five spice powder, ginger and soy sauce and leave for at least 1 hour for flavours to penetrate.

2. Combine the flours and use to coat the chicken.

3. Heat the oil in a wok and deep-fry a few chicken pieces at a time until golden brown. Drain on kitchen paper and keep warm.

4. Pour out almost all the oil you fried the chicken in, leaving 1 tablespoon oil in the wok. Add the plum or hoisin sauce, vinegar, soy sauce, and salt if necessary.

5. Add the chicken pieces and mix thoroughly. When ready to serve, scatter the toasted sesame seeds over the top.

CHICKEN SATAY

✦

HAVING 24-hour hawker stalls on every street corner ensures that no one ever goes hungry out East. Instead of eating a chocolate bar when a bad case of the 'munchies' strikes, the equivalent of only 50p will buy 10 sticks of sizzling, deliciously flavoured morsels of barbecued meat, served with the ever-present chilli sauce or dip peculiar to that particular vendor.

Julian was in gourmet heaven in Thailand. If not out buying loads of clothes in Bangkok (a shopaholic's paradise), he would be gorging himself on pork, squid, or these chicken satays. Once he was just about to bite into a particularly juicy stick of five chunky pieces when Rani pointed out that they were in fact chicken bottoms – a speciality! You may be relieved to know that our recipe uses chicken thighs instead. Serve them with *Saus Kachang* (p.10).

SERVES 4

1½lb (675g) chicken thighs, de-boned and skinned
½ teaspoon ground cinnamon
1 teaspoon ground cumin
1 teaspoon ground coriander
½ teaspoon ground turmeric
1 teaspoon sugar

1 tablespoon salted roasted peanuts, ground
6 spring onions, washed, trimmed and chopped
1 stalk lemon grass, crushed, or the finely grated rind of 1 lemon
2 tablespoons oil

1. Cut the chicken thighs into small, bite-sized pieces.

2. Mix all the remaining ingredients together in a bowl, add the chicken pieces, and marinate for at least 2 hours.

3. If using bamboo sticks, soak them in water for at least an hour before use. Alternatively, you can use metal skewers.

4. Thread the chicken pieces on the skewers, and grill or barbecue until brown and sizzling.

SOUR FRIED CHICKEN

✦

O N THE last day of the children's holiday in Bangkok (we were staying on, to visit relatives in Malaysia), we finally got round to seeking out Rani's birthplace. Armed with directions to Pisanalok House, we went by taxi and stopped at a large stately home. An exhausting hour followed while we traipsed from sentry gate to sentry gate (each one guarded by a machine-gun-armed soldier), brandishing Rani's birth certificate and demanding to be let in.

The midday sun was boiling hot so you can imagine our mortification when we found we had been trying to gain entry to the wrong palace. Instead of going to no. 428 we had stopped at no. 1 (the equivalent of the House of Commons), on the eve of yet another Prime Ministerial resignation. No wonder the soldiers were edgy, although we looked less than terrifying – all dressed in fake designer shorts, trainers, silly straw hats and bum bags!

The kids were hot, bothered and hungry and refused to budge until we found a hawker's stall selling fried chicken to compensate. This is a deceptively easy Thai recipe, excellent for appeasing angry tempers and unpleasant mutterings about the state of our mental health! It's good served with plain boiled rice and mixed fried vegetables.

SERVES 4

4 chicken breasts
1 pint (570ml) oil
5–10 cloves garlic (according to taste), peeled and chopped
1 tablespoon soy sauce

juice of 2 limes
1 tablespoon fish sauce (optional) or extra salt to taste
1 teaspoon sugar
2 red chillies, finely sliced

1. Cut each breast into 8 pieces.

2. Heat the oil in a wok. Fry the chicken until golden brown, then pour off the oil.

3. Add the remaining ingredients, together with 4 tablespoons water, simmer until tender, and serve.

CHICKEN TERIYAKI

✦

THIS IS one of the great Japanese dishes and, once you have eaten it, we are sure you will agree that its reputation is richly deserved. Serve with plain white rice.

SERVES 4

4 × 4oz (110g) chicken breast fillets   1 quantity Quick Teriyaki Sauce (p.7)

1. Slash each chicken fillet deeply with 3 vertical cuts. Put them in a plastic bag with the sauce and leave in the refrigerator for at least 4 hours or overnight, turning once or twice to let the sauce soak in deeply.

2. Cook on a hot barbecue or under a fierce grill, turning frequently and basting with any leftover sauce, for 15–20 minutes until dark brown and cooked through.

VARIATION

✦ Cut the chicken into small cubes and thread them on bamboo sticks (pre-soaked in water for an hour to stop them burning) and this becomes another favourite Japanese dish, Yakitori.

OPPOSITE Singapore Chilli Crab (page 93)

THAI DUCK CURRY

✦

IN THAILAND this curry was served in a young green coconut shell still lined with creamy soft flesh. What joy to eat the delicious meat and then the white coconut meat which was flavoured by the spicy sauce. It's good with some crunchy Fried Onion Flakes (p.10) sprinkled over the top before serving. Accompany with white rice and Thai Red Bean Curry (p.71).

SERVES 3–4

1 × 4½lb (2kg) duckling
2 teaspoons salt
1 teaspoon ground turmeric
2 tablespoons soy sauce
3 onions, peeled and roughly chopped
a 2 inch (5cm) piece ginger, peeled
3 cloves garlic, peeled
3 tablespoons roughly chopped fresh coriander

1 teaspoon black peppercorns, coarsely ground
4 red chillies
2 stalks lemon grass
1 teaspoon *trasi* or *blachan* shrimp paste (optional)
4 tablespoons oil
1 pint (570ml) coconut milk (either 1½ cans or 4oz (110g) coconut cream mixed with water)

1. Cut the duck into 12 pieces, put it in a bowl, and mix with the salt, turmeric and soy sauce. Leave on one side for 30 minutes to allow the flavours to sink into the meat.

2. Place the onion, ginger, garlic, coriander, black pepper, chillies, lemon grass and shrimp paste (if using) in a blender, with 2 tablespoons water, and liquidise to a paste.

3. Heat the oil, fry the spice paste for 2 minutes. Then add the duck pieces and stir over a medium heat for about 4 minutes.

4. Add the coconut milk, bring to the boil, then simmer for about an hour or until the duck is tender.

VARIATION

✦ You can use chicken or red meat just as well. Reduce the cooking time accordingly.

OPPOSITE *Top to bottom:* Braised Pork and Pumpkin (page 112) served with Broccoli in Oyster Sauce (page 74)

SOY BRAISED DUCK

♦

THIS IS a simple Chinese recipe which tastes sensational. All over the Orient, ducks are cooked whole, then cut into very small pieces and served on a bed of rice with chilli sauce and cucumber batons (cut into 2 inch (5cm) lengths) – a favourite dish of office and manual workers alike.

When we were walking down the back streets of Bangkok's Chinatown we came across an entire family – granny, grandad, mum, dad, uncles, aunties, kids, toddlers, babies – sitting cross-legged, chopsticks flying, in an ornate Chinese temple, noisily relishing bowls of duck and rice. Chinese temples are places for eating as well as having your fortune told; for venerating dead ancestors and meeting friends. Not for them the hushed reverence of Christian churches!

SERVES 4–5

1 × 5–5½lb (2.25–2.5kg) duckling
4 spring onions, washed, trimmed and
    chopped
a 2 inch (5cm) piece fresh ginger, peeled
    and grated
6 tablespoons dark soy sauce (thicker than
    light soy sauce but just use 2
    tablespoons more if that's all you have)

3 tablespoons brandy
3 tablespoons brown sugar
1 star anise (optional)

1. Bring 4½ pints (2.5 litres) water to the boil in a very large pan. Add the duck carefully (hold it by its neck and bottom), chest down, and boil for 3 minutes. Turn it over and boil for a further 3 minutes.

2. Take out the duck, strain off a little less than half the water (save to add to soup), then add all the remaining ingredients. Bring to the boil, then add the duck, cover and simmer for 1–1½ hours or until the duck is tender, turning several times during cooking.

3. Remove the duck, cut into small pieces and serve with the sauce. (If you like a thicker sauce, just boil until reduced to a thick 'jam', taking care not to let it burn.)

EASY HONEY-SPICED ROAST DUCK

✦

WE LOVE roast duck – it is our favourite dish. When taken out by our kids (now all earning money and able to reward us for all the loving care and attention we have showered on them from birth!), we invariably steer them towards Chinatown. They would like us to be more adventurous and try other cuisines. We sometimes do. But, to be honest, we like to eat rice! After considering every item on the menu, costing it out to the last penny, bemoaning the expense and how we are getting ripped off, we nearly always order some sort of roast duck.

One of our favourite restaurants in London is Wong Kei's in Wardour Street, where the service is appallingly abrupt though super-fast. You are forced to sit rubbing shoulders with anyone who walks in off the street but you can eat well for about a fiver! Do try it – it's an experience you shouldn't miss but only if you have a good sense of humour.

Serve this dish with boiled white rice, Chinese Greens (p.70), and a dipping sauce (2 tablespoons soy sauce mixed with 1 small chopped fresh chilli).

SERVES 4–5

1 × 5–5½lb (2.25–2.5kg) duckling
2½ teaspoons five spice powder
1 tablespoon salt

2 tablespoons runny honey mixed with
½ teaspoon ground cinnamon

1. Wash and dry the duck inside and out but leave it a bit damp so that the spice will cling to it.

2. Mix the spice powder and salt together, then rub well into the duck both inside and out. Leave the duck on a dish in the fridge uncovered overnight on the lowest shelf (you want it to dry out but not to drip onto anything).

3. Preheat the oven to 220°C/425°F/Gas Mark 7. Cook the duck for 10 minutes, then turn over and roast for a further 10 minutes. Reduce to 190°C/375°F/Gas Mark 5 and cook for 40 minutes, turning once during this time. Take the duck out and turn the heat back up to 220°C/425°F/Gas Mark 7.

4. Brush the duck with the honey mixture, put back in the oven and roast for a final 10 minutes or so, on its back, until deliciously brown. Cut into small pieces and serve.

Eggs

WHEN we were recently in Bangkok we saw food-sellers sitting on small stools with baskets by their sides in which were hundreds and hundreds of tiny, beautiful, speckled quail's eggs. These would be fried in oil, ten at a time, in a round iron mould, a bit like an egg poacher. The cooked eggs would then be put into a plastic bag, a slosh of sweet chilli sauce poured over, and a bamboo stick presented to spear the delicious mouthfuls.

Because so many Oriental people keep chickens, ways of cooking eggs (with their valuable protein) are legion. We love eating omelettes with rice and plain hot water, spiced up with either a spoonful of soy sauce or plain with a teaspoon of *tung choi* (preserved Chinese garlic shoots). Spicy omelettes are very popular, with meat, fish, prawn or vegetable fillings. Also popular are eggs which have been boiled, then gently simmered in curry sauce.

The only thing you *won't* find in the Orient is a cheese omelette. Indians eat a soft cheese made by adding vinegar or lemon juice to milk to curdle it, then draining it of whey (liquid) and pressing it to make *paneer*. It is rare to find any form of cheese in any other Oriental cuisine.

SAMBOL GORENG EGGS
Indonesian Spicy Eggs

✦

SAMBOL GORENG is a basic sauce in which you can cook small pieces of meat, liver, prawns or vegetables.

Tamarind is now becoming easy to find in good grocery shops or even supermarkets. Don't be put off if you can't get it – it has a distinctive sweet sour flavour but Worcester sauce is close.

SERVES 4

8 hen's eggs or 24 quail's eggs
3 cloves garlic, peeled
a 1 inch (2.5cm) piece galangal
    (optional), peeled
1 onion, peeled and roughly chopped
2 chillies
1 teaspoon salt
3 tablespoons oil
3 tablespoons tomato ketchup
1 medium tomato, cut into small pieces

2 bay leaves
grated rind of a lemon
10fl oz (275ml) canned coconut milk
1 tablespoon jaggery (palm sugar) or
    brown sugar
1 teaspoon tamarind concentrate or 1 tea-
    spoon tamarind pulp mixed with 3
    tablespoons hot water and strained, *or*
    1 tablespoon lemon juice and 1 tea-
    spoon Worcester sauce

1. Hard-boil and shell the eggs. Cut the hen's eggs into quarters. If using quail's eggs, leave whole.

2. Put the garlic, galangal if using, onion, chillies and salt in a liquidiser and process to a paste.

3. Heat the oil in a saucepan, then fry the paste, stirring all the time until it gives off a wonderful aroma and looks cooked. Add the ketchup, tomato, bay leaves, lemon rind and coconut milk, and stir.

4. Simmer for 3 minutes, then add the eggs very carefully and simmer for a further 10 minutes. Stir in the sugar, and the tamarind or the lemon juice and Worcester sauce mixture. Check the seasoning and serve.

WHOLE FRIED EGGS WITH PRAWN STUFFING

✦

THE FIRST word Justin, Rani's firstborn, spoke, after Dada and Mum, was 'gags' – his interpretation of 'eggs'. As the only baby in the family for some years, we made him repeat this magical word over and over again, until he was heartily sick of it and refused to perform – even to get his favourite soft-boiled egg and bread-and-butter soldiers. Nevertheless, he still loves eggs, and this special whole fried egg recipe is one of his favourites. Try serving with Sweet Garlic and Chilli Sauce (p.12) or Easy Peanut and Orange Dip (p.11).

SERVES 4–5

8 hard-boiled eggs

12oz (350g) cooked prawns, chopped

2 premium pork sausages, skins removed

1 tablespoon fish sauce or 1 teaspoon salt and 1 teaspoon soy sauce

2 spring onions, washed, trimmed and chopped

1 teaspoon chopped fresh coriander (optional)

2 tablespoons canned coconut milk

a pinch of sugar

¼ teaspoon ground white pepper

1¾ pints (1 litre) oil (for deep-frying)

For the batter

4oz (110g) self-raising flour

1 teaspoon salt

a pinch of sugar

2 tablespoons oil

1. Shell the eggs, cut each one in half, remove the yolks and mash them. Add all the ingredients, except the oil and the batter ingredients, to the yolks and use to stuff the egg white halves so each half resembles a whole egg. Refrigerate for 1 hour until hard.

2. Whisk all the batter ingredients together with 4fl oz (110ml) water, or use a blender. Dip each stuffed egg into the batter and fry in hot oil in a wok until golden brown and crispy. Cut in half vertically so each half contains white and stuffing, and place face down on a plate and serve with a spicy dipping sauce.

THAI SAVOURY MEAT OMELETTE

✦

TRADITIONALLY made with pork, you can also make this omelette with other meats, minced prawns or even puréed aubergines (see below). A versatile dish, it makes an unusual breakfast or light supper, and is great eaten cold for a picnic or buffet, especially if it is stuffed in a *puri* (p.44).

SERVES 4

8oz (225g) minced pork
2 cloves garlic, peeled and crushed
2 tablespoons oil
8 large eggs
2 teaspoons salt
3 spring onions, washed, trimmed and
    finely chopped

1 tablespoon chopped fresh coriander plus
    an extra teaspoon for garnish
½ teaspoon chilli powder
¼ teaspoon ground turmeric
a pinch of sugar (optional)

1. Fry the pork and garlic in 1 tablespoon oil until it just changes colour. Leave on one side to cool.

2. Beat the eggs with the salt, then add all the ingredients except for the remaining tablespoon of oil and the extra coriander. Heat 1 teaspoon oil in a heavy-based frying pan and pour a quarter of the egg mixture into it. Make an omelette, turning until both sides are brown. Place on a plate. Repeat 3 more times, stacking each omelette on top of the one before.

3. Serve sprinkled with the extra coriander leaves and slice like a pie.

VARIATION

✦ Prick one large aubergine all over with a skewer (to stop it exploding), then bake in a hot oven until it collapses. Scrape out the purée and use in place of the pork.

EGG AND CHILLI CURRY

✦

THIS IS perfect for vegetarians or for when you feel like a lighter meal. Besides being very tasty it looks so good, with the halved eggs peeping up from the rich, spicy sauce. Sprinkle some Fried Onion Flakes (p.10) over the top before serving with plain white rice, *Roti Canai* (p.42) or Stringhopper Pilau (p.63). A sambol made from 1lb (450g) tomatoes, 1 medium onion and ½ cucumber, all diced, and seasoned with ½ teaspoon sugar, 2 teaspoons vinegar, 1 teaspoon salt and 1 teaspoon chilli powder, would make this a very tasty vegetarian meal.

SERVES 4–6

4 eggs
1 large onion, peeled and roughly chopped
2 cloves garlic, peeled
3 teaspoons crushed dried chillies
a pinch of grated nutmeg
3 tablespoons oil

½ teaspoon *blachan* or dried shrimp paste (optional)
1 teaspoon sugar
½ teaspoon chopped lemon grass or grated lemon rind
8fl oz (225ml) canned coconut milk

1. Hard-boil the eggs, shell and halve them. Set aside.

2. Put the onion, garlic, chillies and nutmeg into a liquidiser and blend to a paste.

3. Heat the oil in a saucepan, fry the paste for 3 minutes, then add the rest of the ingredients and bring to the boil.

4. Turn the heat down to a simmer, add the halved eggs, cut-side down, and cook gently for 5 minutes or until the gravy begins to thicken.

EGG AND CRAB SCRAMBLE

✦

IT IS sometimes quite strange when cultures collide. Our Malaysian cousins are very Westernised but one custom which did take us aback, when we ate out, was to have communal plates heaped with separate dishes, which everyone tucked into at once. Perhaps a lot of this hesitancy came from feelings peeved (they are so much more adept with their chopsticks that we were left behind – one mouthful to their ten!). But eating this Chinese version of scrambled eggs from a plate shared with other people seemed a bit unhygienic, and we never quite got the hang of getting a slippery mouthful of egg to our lips! Try this recipe though – it is very good served with plain white rice.

SERVES 4–5

3 tablespoons oil
1 × ½ inch (1cm) slice fresh ginger
1 tablespoon sherry
1 teaspoon salt
¼ teaspoon ground white pepper
8 eggs

3 tablespoons washed, trimmed and chopped spring onions
3oz (75g) lightly cooked petits pois
8oz (225g) fresh, frozen or canned crab-meat or the same quantity of crabsticks, finely chopped

1. Use the oil to coat a wok, then rub the ginger slice all over the surface, to flavour the oil. Throw away the ginger.

2. Put the sherry, salt, pepper and eggs in a bowl and beat together.

3. Stir-fry the spring onions and cooked peas for 2 minutes in the ginger-oiled wok, add the crab and stir briefly to heat through. Then add the egg mixture and stir with a fork or a pair of chopsticks to scramble.

4. Tip out into a warmed serving dish and serve immediately while still creamy and hot.

Fish and Seafood

THIS IS most definitely the most popular protein in the Orient and is it any wonder? Walk through any market place in South-East Asia and you will see huge sharks grinning with small, malevolent eyes; giant sides of tuna, the blood red meat in concentric layers like some living tree trunk; small fish and large fish, all the colours of the rainbow. Walk on, and there is amazing red snapper with black spots; black pomfret which makes such good eating; prawns and shrimps and clams and cockles; huge squid; small tender cuttlefish; octopus like gnarled rope, their many arms twined sinuously around each other in a death embrace; bad-tempered crabs, their pincers raised in defiance; lobsters much quieter, waiting for an opportunity to snap their tails and make their escape. The list is endless and we would stand mesmerised, watching the shiny knives wielded by dextrous hands which could turn a huge pile of flapping fish into neat fillets and cutlets in no time at all.

We went to Trengganu on the east coast of Malaysia to see the giant turtles lay their eggs on the nearby beach. Following some ancient instinct, these huge reptiles are thought to swim many thousands of miles to return to the very spot where they first entered the sea to lay their own eggs. We were fortunate enough to see the fishermen come back in the very early hours of the morning when the sky was a delicate blush pink from the rising sun. Their boats have ornately carved mastheads called *bongau* and it was a joy to behold them sailing in – an exotic flotilla laden with the harvest of the seas.

In Sri Lanka an essential ingredient in cooking – not just for fish but vegetables and meat too – is maldive fish, a dried salted fish which we put into everything. The Malays use *ikan bilis* (salted anchovies or fry of other fish) which they crumble into curries; while the Thais and Indonesians rely heavily on fish sauce, again made from anchovies. Burma and all the other Oriental countries also make use of shrimps – either salted and ground to a powder or made into malodorous blocks of *blachan* (shrimp paste).

SINGAPORE CHILLI CRAB

✦

A CULINARY masterpiece – get ready for one of the best meals of your life! But this is not a dish to serve when the boss and partner come to dinner – definitely a time for bibs, plenty of paper tissues, fingerbowls and deliciously rude slurping noises!

SERVES 4

2 X 2lb (900g) cooked crabs, cleaned
2 cloves garlic, peeled
a 1 inch (2.5cm) piece ginger, peeled
2 fresh chillies
1 teaspoon *blachan* or shrimp paste
  (optional)
2 stalks lemon grass
4 tablespoons oil

about 8 spring onions, washed, trimmed
  and chopped
6 tablespoons tomato ketchup
1 teaspoon tomato purée
½ teaspoon hot chilli powder
1 tablespoon brown sugar
1 teaspoon lemon juice
a few fresh coriander leaves, chopped
  (optional)

1. Ask your fishmonger to clean the crabs for you, then cut the bodies into 4 pieces. Break off the claws and feet, and crack the claws with a hammer – just enough to let the sauce get in.

2. Put the garlic, ginger, chillies, shrimp paste if using, and lemon grass in a blender, and process with a little water until it becomes a paste.

3. Heat the oil in a wok or large saucepan and fry the paste until fragrant. Add the rest of the ingredients, except the coriander if using, 15fl oz (425ml) water, and the crabs, and keep turning until the crabs are thoroughly coated with the spicy sauce.

4. Sprinkle with a few chopped fresh coriander leaves if liked, and serve.

THAI FISH CAKES

✦

THAILAND is the land of fast food. On every corner there will be a group of people busy stirring cauldrons of steaming noodles or deep-frying some of these very popular fish cakes. Three of these popped into a plastic bag, with a teaspoon of seemingly innocuous but deadly hot chilli sauce in the bottom, make for good munching while examining 'genuine Lolex' (Rolex) watches for $5 in a night street market.

Thai Fish Cakes make a good snack or starter and are excellent served with dipping sauces, such as equal amounts of tomato ketchup and chilli sauce mixed together, or soy sauce with chopped fresh green chillies.

SERVES 4

1–2 fresh chillies

2 cloves garlic, peeled

1 stalk lemon grass, crushed, or the grated rind of 1 lime

2 tablespoons Thai fish sauce *or* 2 table-spoons soy sauce and 1 finely chopped anchovy

1lb (450g) fresh white fish fillets, cut into cubes

4 tablespoons canned coconut milk or 4 tablespoons desiccated coconut mixed with 4 tablespoons hot milk and strained

2 large eggs, beaten

oil

1. Put the chillies, garlic, lemon grass or lime rind, and fish sauce or anchovy/soy sauce in a food processor and process to a smooth paste.

2. Add the fish and process again. Stir in the coconut milk and just enough beaten egg to form a stiff mixture. Leave for a few hours, or overnight, until the mixture becomes firm enough to form into balls.

3. Shape into small flat cakes and fry in hot oil until crisp and brown. Turn over and fry until brown on the other side.

4. Drain on plenty of crumpled kitchen paper, and serve.

SRI LANKAN FISH CURRY

✦

THIS IS a lovely curry, sweetish because of the tomato, yet hot and savoury. Serve with Spicy Green Leaf Purée (p.73), and plain white rice or Parathas (p.46).

SERVES 4

1lb (450g) firm fish steaks (tuna, mackerel or haddock), cut into 2 inch (5cm) chunks
1 teaspoon salt
1 teaspoon ground turmeric
3 tablespoons oil
1 large onion, peeled and chopped
2 cloves garlic, peeled and chopped

2 teaspoons grated ginger
1 large red beef tomato, cut into chunks
1 tablespoon curry powder
1 teaspoon chilli powder
10fl oz (275ml) canned coconut milk
2 curry leaves and a 1 inch (2.5cm) piece *rampe* or pandanus leaf (optional)
1 teaspoon lemon juice

1. Rub the fish with the salt and turmeric. Fry in 1 tablespoon oil until brown, and set aside.

2. Put the onion, garlic, ginger and tomato into a liquidiser and blend to a paste.

3. Fry this paste in the remaining 2 tablespoons oil until the oil begins to separate and a lovely aroma is released. Add the curry powder and chilli powder, and fry for a few minutes more.

4. Add the coconut milk, and *rampe* if using, and simmer for 3 minutes. Add the fish and spoon over the sauce. Take off the heat, stir in the lemon juice, and serve.

PRAWNS WITH SWEET BEAN SAUCE

✦

A DELICIOUS dish – quite different but so quick and easy. Use fresh uncooked prawns or shrimp if possible; if not, large pink prawns in their shells.

Serve with Steamed Noodle Packets (p.64) or plain boiled white rice and Healthy Stir-Fried Vegetables (p.75).

SERVES 4–5

2 tablespoons oil

2 spring onions, washed, trimmed and finely chopped

2 slices ginger, grated

2 cloves garlic, peeled and crushed

1 fresh chilli

2 tablespoons water chestnuts, drained and chopped small

4 tablespoons chicken stock

2 tablespoons sweet bean sauce or hoisin sauce

1 tablespoon soy sauce

2 teaspoons rice wine or sherry

1 teaspoon sugar

salt (to taste)

1lb (450g) prawns

1. Heat the oil in a wok and fry the spring onions, ginger, garlic, chilli and water chestnuts for 2 minutes. Add the rest of the ingredients, except the prawns, and simmer for a further 3 minutes.

2. Add the prawns and either cook until done; or, if using cooked prawns, heat through thoroughly.

COCKLE, MUSSEL AND CLAM MASALA

✦

ALTHOUGH it is hard to beat plain shellfish enlivened with chilli dips or melted butter, we also love it served with a spicy sauce as in this recipe. Try it – we're sure you'll find it 'moreish' too!

SERVES 3–4

2lb (900g) mixed shellfish (e.g. mussels, cockles, clams, even prawns), or 1lb (450g) frozen seafood, defrosted	3 cloves
	3 red chillies
	2 cloves garlic, peeled
2 onions, peeled and chopped	3 tablespoons vinegar
1 tablespoon grated fresh ginger	4 tablespoons canned coconut milk
2oz (50g) de-seeded tamarind paste	2 tablespoons oil
1 teaspoon ground turmeric	½ bunch fresh coriander, washed and
1 teaspoon ground coriander	chopped

1. If using fresh shellfish, scrub the shells well in plenty of fresh running water and discard any damaged ones.

2. Grind everything, except the oil, shellfish and fresh coriander, to a smooth masala paste in a liquidiser, adding a little water if necessary.

3. Fry the masala in the oil, stirring well until it begins to 'split' (a fancy name for when the oil begins to separate).

4. Taste and add a little sugar if the tamarind is particularly sour.

5. Add the washed shellfish and cover; the shells will open in the steam (discard any that don't). If using prepared seafood, add now. Remove the saucepan lid and sprinkle the coriander over the top.

VARIATION

✦ A highly unorthodox splash of white wine adds a wonderful eye-opening note to the sauce.

PRAWN ROLLS WITH MUSHROOMS, HAM AND BAMBOO SHOOTS

✦

USE LARGE, fresh tiger prawns for this dish and make your guests' or family's eyes pop out. It's quite stunning and so easy to make; you will need a steamer and 8 wooden cocktail sticks.

Although we do not normally serve starters in the East (all the savoury dishes are put on the table at the same time), we have suggested, throughout this book, when a particular dish might be suitable as a starter. This is one of those dishes, which when served on fresh lettuce or spinach leaves will leave prawn cocktail standing at the starting gate!

SERVES 4

8 large uncooked prawns, peeled and cleaned, with heads removed but tails still on

2½oz (75g) bamboo shoots, finely shredded

½oz (15g) ham, finely sliced

1 oyster or black mushroom, washed and finely shredded

½ small carrot, cut into fine strips

1 small green chilli, finely shredded

2oz (50g) beansprouts

2oz (50g) mustard greens or spinach, finely shredded

1 teaspoon sesame oil and 1 teaspoon vegetable oil mixed together

½ teaspoon salt

½ teaspoon sugar

½ teaspoon ground white pepper

1 teaspoon cornflour mixed to a cream with 1 tablespoon water

1. Cut down the dark line which runs down the back of each prawn (throw the line away – this is the digestive tract) and cut the prawn almost in half through the middle. Lay flat like a butterfly.

2. Mix the bamboo shoots, ham, mushroom, carrot, chilli, beansprouts and greens together and place a teaspoonful in the middle of each prawn. Roll up each prawn towards the tail (see illustration opposite), and use a cocktail stick to secure. Keep leftover filling to one side.

3. Place the prawn rolls in a steamer and steam over boiling water for 4 minutes. Keep warm.

4. Heat the oils in a wok and stir-fry the leftover filling for 2 minutes. Add the salt, sugar, pepper and cornflour mixture, check the seasoning and cook until the sauce thickens.

5. Place the prawn rolls on a warm dish, spoon over the sauce, and serve.

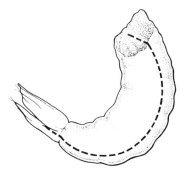

1 cut the prawn almost in two and remove the intestine

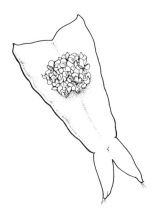

2 flatten the prawn, add filling in the middle

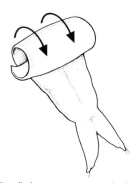

4 use a toothpick to close

3 roll the prawn towards the tail

IKAN ACAR
Malay Pickled Fish

✦

MACKEREL is a wonderful fish – cheap, full of protein, no small nasty bones and, best of all, no horrible scales to remove. *Acar* means pickle sauce – in this recipe the spicy sauce is poured over fried fish, then left to mature overnight.

Eat it cold with *Roti Canai* (p.42) or crusty bread for a very tasty Oriental snack, or serve it with a rice dish like Kichiri (p.55).

SERVES 4

1lb (450g) mackerel fillets
1 teaspoon salt
1 teaspoon ground turmeric
6 tablespoons oil
1 large onion, peeled, cut into quarters
  and then very thinly sliced
4 tablespoons vinegar
2 tablespoons jaggery (palm sugar) or
  dark brown sugar
8 cashew nuts

2 chillies, sliced
a 2 inch (5cm) piece fresh ginger, peeled
2 cloves garlic, peeled
1 teaspoon mustard seeds (optional)
½ teaspoon black peppercorns
½ teaspoon mustard powder mixed to a
  paste with 1 teaspoon vinegar
1 teaspoon ground cumin
½ teaspoon chilli powder

1. Rub the fish with the salt and turmeric and leave for at least 2 hours. Fry on both sides in the oil until golden brown, then remove with a slotted spoon, allowing the excess oil to drain back into the pan. Place in a large flat glass or ceramic dish, cover with half the sliced onions and leave on one side.

2. Put the vinegar and sugar in a pan, with 8 tablespoons water, and boil until syrupy. Set aside.

3. Put the cashew nuts, chillies, ginger, remaining onion, garlic, mustard seeds if using, and black peppercorns in a food processor, together with a little of the vinegar syrup, and process to a paste. Add the mustard mix, cumin and chilli powder and the remaining vinegar syrup.

4. Pour over the fish and onions, refrigerate and leave overnight before serving.

HOT THAI-STYLE SPICY SCALLOPS

✦

SCALLOPS are the most delicate of shellfish and, because of their cost and tender texture, they are usually treated with reverence. You can now buy frozen baby scallops in good supermarkets. This recipe treats them quite robustly but, served with *Nasi Goreng* (p.53), we hope you will agree that they stand up to it well.

This is about the only recipe in which we tell you to discard the chilli seeds. Brought up by a frugal mother, we usually reduce the amount of chillies instead. However this sauce should be delicate and not too over-poweringly hot.

SERVES 4

16 medium-sized scallops
2oz (50g) butter, melted
2 tablespoons lime juice
1 teaspoon chopped garlic
1 tablespoon chopped spring onions
1 teaspoon chopped galangal or ginger

1 tablespoon chopped fresh coriander
½ teaspoon salt
½ teaspoon ground white pepper
1 small fresh chilli, de-seeded and
   chopped

1. Mix all the ingredients together and leave for about 20 minutes for the flavours to develop.

2. Preheat the grill and cook under a medium heat until just done (about 10–12 minutes). Watch the scallops carefully – they need minimal cooking to remain tender and sweet.

FRIED AROMATIC SQUID
✦

THIS IS an eye-catching dish, with the diamond-cut squid looking like miniature porcupines in a colourful sauce of green leaves and red chillies. Try serving it with boiled white rice, Chinese Greens (p.70), or Broccoli in Oyster Sauce (p.74) for a quick, well-balanced meal.

SERVES 3–4

2 large squid hoods
4 tablespoons oil
2 spring onions, washed, trimmed and
   cut into thin strips
1 slice ginger, peeled and grated
1 red chilli, cut into fine strips
1 teaspoon salt

½ tablespoon rice wine, ginger wine or
   sherry
2 teaspoons cornflour mixed to a cream
   with 2 teaspoons soy sauce
3 sprigs flat-leaf Chinese parsley or fresh
   coriander, chopped
½ tablespoon sesame oil

1. Wash the squid and strip off the skin. Cut open and lay flat, skin-side uppermost. Using a very sharp knife, cut diagonal lines close together, but not right through to the other side. Then cut similar lines in the opposite direction. You will end up with tiny diamond-shaped cuts all over the surface of the squid. Alternatively you could use a pair of kitchen scissors to make random V-shaped snips over the whole surface, all facing the same direction. After you have scored or snipped the squid, cut into bite-sized pieces.

2. Half-fill a saucepan with water, bring to the boil, then drop in the squid pieces and cook for 1 minute. Remove immediately and keep warm.

3. Heat the oil in a wok, and stir-fry the spring onions, ginger and chilli for 1 minute. Add the squid, salt, wine or sherry, cornflour mixture and parsley or coriander, and stir-fry for a further 2 minutes until the sauce thickens.

4. Sprinkle the sesame oil over the top, and serve.

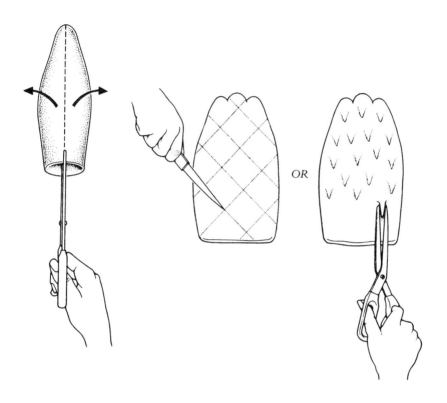

OR

Meat

THE ORIENT is blessed with relatively unpolluted seas and oceans teeming with such a profusion of fish and seafood that meat tends to take second place on national menus.

Meat also tends to be expensive in comparison with fish, so it is usually prepared in ways that make a little go a long way. One of our brothers-in-law was teasing us about the trouble we have with our weight, and he said it was because we were combining Eastern and Western diets and taking the worst of both. After we had finished battering him and rubbishing his argument, we slowly came round to agreeing with him, albeit reluctantly.

In Bangkok for example, everyone is about a size eight (including the men), although they seem to eat all day long. It is rare to see a really fat Thai. But if you look closer at their diet (as well as that of other Orientals, and even the Sri Lankans, our father's people), you find that they all eat a large amount of rice, a goodly portion of vegetables and a very small amount of meat, poultry or fish – not much more than a couple of ounces. Here in the West we eat a Westerner's kingsize portion of protein (an average 6–8oz (175–225g) helping) with a huge Oriental portion of rice – a calorie and cholesterol disaster!

We are now trying to return to healthier traditional Oriental eating patterns and have reduced our meat intake accordingly. In most of our recipes we cut our meat into very small cubes or strips (which also cuts down on cooking time) and prepare deliciously spicy sauces to complement rather than blanket the flavour of the beef, lamb, pork or game.

SPICED INDONESIAN FRIED BEEF SLICES
✦

WE HAVE adapted this recipe from one given to us by a lady we recently met on a 30-hour train journey from Bangkok to Kuala Lumpur. This dish comes from Indonesia and she said she ate it served on banana leaves from makeshift wooden pushcarts. To attract customers, the seller bangs together two lengths of bamboo, producing a resonant 'tock tock', while he shouts out his wares.

It takes a little preparation but is well worth the extra effort – believe us! It reminds us a little of our Sri Lankan favourite, Beef Smoore, which we included in our first book, *Tiger Lily – Flavours of the Orient*.

SERVES 4–6

1½lb (675g) beef topside
3 cloves
a 2 inch (5cm) cinnamon stick
½ teaspoon grated nutmeg
1 teaspoon salt
1 pint (570ml) oil
a few fresh coriander leaves
2–4 tomatoes, sliced

For the spice paste
4 red chillies

a 1 inch (2.5cm) piece fresh ginger, peeled and sliced
a 1 inch (2.5cm) piece galangal, peeled and sliced (optional)
3 teaspoons whole coriander seeds, crushed
2 teaspoons black peppercorns, crushed
a 1 inch (2.5cm) piece fresh turmeric root or 1 teaspoon ground turmeric
1 tablespoon tomato purée

1. Put all the spice paste ingredients into a food processor and process to a paste. Set aside.

2. Put the joint of beef in a deep saucepan with the cloves, cinnamon, nutmeg, salt and 2½ pints (1.5 litres) water. Simmer until the beef is half-cooked (about 45 minutes). Take the meat out (save the stock for later), allow to cool, then cut into thin slices about 2 inches (5cm) wide.

3. Return the beef slices and the spice paste to a saucepan, add all the stock and simmer, uncovered, for 45–60 minutes, until the beef is tender and the stock is thick. If the beef is tender and there is still too much liquid, remove the beef slices to a plate and boil the sauce, stirring to prevent the bottom catching, until it is reduced to a thick purée.

4. Drain the beef, then deep-fry in hot oil until brown. Remove from the pan with a slotted spoon, dish out on a plate, pour the sauce over and garnish with fresh coriander leaves and slices of tomato.

TWELVE-MINUTE THAI RED BEEF CURRY

✦

THIS IS a Thai-style sweet and sour curry which is so simple to make. Just prepare your curry paste, fry the beef, add the paste and some coconut milk, then simmer until cooked. If you use steak, it should take not much longer than 12 minutes! On the other hand, using economical stewing or braising beef will only add an extra 10 minutes or so.

Most of these ingredients can now be found in supermarkets. And some are starting to stock excellent small bottles of puréed ginger, garlic, chillies and even coriander and lemon grass. Don't be put off if you are short of one or two ingredients. Make the dish anyway, taste and season to your own requirements.

SERVES 3–4

2 stalks lemon grass or 2 teaspoons lemon grass purée

4 spring onions, washed, trimmed and roughly chopped

2 cloves garlic, peeled, or 2 teaspoons garlic purée

a 2 inch (5cm) piece ginger or 1 teaspoon ginger purée

1 tablespoon soy sauce

2 red chillies or 2 teaspoons red chilli paste

2 teaspoons *blachan* or shrimp paste (optional)

1 teaspoon coarsely ground black pepper

1 teaspoon ground turmeric

1 teaspoon ground coriander

2 tablespoons oil

1lb (450g) braising beef, cut into small ¾ inch (2cm) chunks

7fl oz (200ml) canned coconut milk

1 lime, washed, cut in half and then into thin slices (keep the skin but get rid of the seeds)

1. Put all the ingredients, except the oil, beef, coconut milk and lime, into a food processor and blend until smooth. Use some of the coconut milk to thin down a little if it gets too thick.

2. Heat the oil in a saucepan, add the beef and stir-fry for 2 minutes. Add the paste and fry again for another 3 minutes.

3. Add the coconut milk and lime slices and simmer for a further 10–15 minutes, stirring occasionally until the beef is tender. Add a little extra water if the sauce reduces too much.

VARIATION

✦ Decorate, if you wish, with a teaspoon of toasted desiccated coconut and some grated carrot mixed with a little sugar, salt, vinegar and chilli powder.

TIGER LILY LAMB KEBABS

✦

BROWSING in our local supermarket recently, we saw a number of bamboo sticks with what looked like a minced meat mixture surrounding them. These were labelled Chinese and Greek satays and Indian-style kebabs and we immediately bought some. What a disappointment – to us they tasted bland, over-processed and a pale imitation of the sticks we could buy back East.

Why not try our recipe instead, which works equally well with pork or beef? It's best to buy the meat in cubes and mince your own, to avoid getting palmed off with fatty and dubious cuts.

Served with pitta bread, or rice and a green salad, these kebabs are juicy and tasty. Eat them as soon after cooking as possible for the best taste, though they can be served warm or heated (once only please!) for a few seconds in a microwave.

MAKES about 24; enough for 4

1lb (450g) boneless lamb, cut into cubes	1 tablespoon chopped fresh coriander
2 cloves garlic, peeled and crushed	leaves or parsley
1 teaspoon salt	juice of 1 lemon
1 teaspoon ground black pepper	2 tablespoons ground rice
2 teaspoons each ground turmeric, cumin,	1 egg, beaten
coriander and chilli powder	1 teaspoon oil

1. Soak 24 bamboo sticks in water for at least 1 hour.

2. Mince the lamb finely with a very sharp knife or in a food processor. Take care to cut the meat into cubes and watch carefully when chopping by machine. (Rani lost a processor by burning out the motor – long sinews of pork wrapped themselves around the blades and ruined the machine.)

3. Place all the ingredients, except the egg and oil, in a bowl, and mix well.

4. Add just enough beaten egg to bind the mixture together – it must not be wet or it will slide off the bamboo sticks.

5. Wet your hands and mould some of the kebab mixture around each stick. Cover the end of the stick and mould the mixture about half to two-thirds of the way down. Continue until all the sticks and mixture are used up.

6. Grill or barbecue, turning once, until brown and sizzling. Brush with oil occasionally.

MADURAN BEEF OR LAMB SATAY

✦

WE SPENT many a pleasant evening 'shopping until we dropped' on our last visit to Bangkok. The kids would disappear at the crack of dawn, only reappearing to deposit armfuls of clothes and trinkets on the bed before going out again. We were most impressed by this diligence, particularly as we tend to find it a chore to get them out of bed in normal circumstances. Street stalls came in very handy during this 'shopping frenzy'. We could purchase satay of almost every description for about 15 pence a stick.

When we got home, we missed these tasty snacks so we rooted through old recipes passed down through the family and found this one – from the island of Madura, north-east of Java – which met Johnny's exacting standards. The beef or lamb is cut into smaller chunks than usual so the flavours soak right through, and the meat cooks in a very short time. If you use fennel, the satay will have a deliciously different, aniseedy taste and aroma.

SERVES 4–6

1 X 2lb (900g) leg of lamb, cut into
  ¾ inch (2cm) cubes
1 tablespoon lime or lemon juice
grated rind of 1 lime or lemon
1 teaspoon coriander seeds, ground
½ teaspoon black peppercorns, crushed
¼ teaspoon ground fennel (optional)

8 tablespoons dark soy sauce
2 tablespoons jaggery (palm sugar) or
  dark brown sugar
4 spring onions, washed, trimmed and
  sliced
½ fresh chilli, chopped (optional)

1. Soak the meat cubes overnight in a mixture of all the ingredients except the spring onions and fresh chilli.

2. Thread the meat onto wooden skewers soaked for 2 hours in water beforehand so they are less likely to burn.

3. Barbecue or grill, turning halfway, until the satays are dark brown yet still juicy. My goodness, the smell will drive you crazy!

4. Boil the leftover marinade with a little water, then allow to cool. Add the spring onions and a little chopped fresh chilli if liked, and use as a dipping sauce.

BARBECUED BUTTERFLY OF LAMB

✦

THIS recipe calls for a whole boned leg of lamb, opened out flat to resemble the wings of a butterfly. Brushed with a spicy marinade, and then grilled or barbecued, it makes a spectacular dish and also goes a long way. Serve it with rice, *Puris* (p.44) or *Parathas* (p.46), a number of fresh salads, Mango Acharu (p.26), and Dipping Sauces and Seasonings (p.14).

In the Caribbean, locals often have an early-morning swim in the warm sea, enjoying the miles of deserted golden sands before the arrival of swarms of flies and tourists. The pre-work swimmers begin to show up as early as 5 or 6 a.m., and in their wake come the traders offering ice-cold canned drinks, coconuts, and of course food to satisfy hungry appetites. Together with *rotis*, Jamaican patties, fried chicken and fish, there will usually be a version of jerk meat or this delicious lamb on sale.

SERVES 8–10

1 X 4lb (1.8kg) leg of lamb, boned and opened out flat

3 teaspoons salt

2 teaspoons ground black pepper

½ small fresh Scotch Bonnet chilli, very finely chopped, or 2 teaspoons Encona hot chilli pepper sauce

3 tablespoons lemon juice

1 teaspoon dried thyme

1 small sprig fresh rosemary or 1 teaspoon dried rosemary

2 cloves garlic, peeled and crushed

2 tablespoons oil

1 teaspoon runny honey

2 teaspoons rum (optional)

2 tablespoons melted butter

1. Wipe the lamb with some kitchen paper, then make deep horizontal cuts on both sides, taking care not to cut right the way through. This will let the marinade soak deep into the meat.

2. Mix all the ingredients, except the butter, together, and use to brush all over both sides of the meat. Wrap in kitchen foil and refrigerate for at least 4 hours to allow the flavours to develop.

3. Grill or, even better, barbecue over charcoal. If using the barbecue, throw a handful of rosemary and a used lemon skin into the charcoal to flavour the meat even more.

4. Cut into wafer-thin slices and enjoy!

SRI LANKAN VENISON AND LIVER CURRY

✦

THESE days, more and more people are starting to enjoy eating tasty, healthy, super-lean game. Venison and even ostrich, wild boar, kangaroo and crocodile are now appearing in supermarkets. Venison is tender and similar to beef, so any favourite beef recipes can be adapted.

This dish, with its mixture of meat and liver, is deliciously different. If you're not keen on the taste of liver, like most of our kids, just use more venison. It's also good using pork, beef or lamb instead.

SERVES 4

2 large onions, peeled and roughly chopped
4 cloves garlic, peeled
2 teaspoons grated ginger
2 stalks lemon grass, roughly chopped
1 teaspoon freshly ground black pepper
1 teaspoon ground cumin
2 teaspoons ground coriander
½ teaspoon ground turmeric

1 teaspoon ground cloves
1 teaspoon ground cinnamon
1 teaspoon chilli powder
1 teaspoon salt
1lb (450g) venison, cut into chunks
8oz (225g) lamb's liver, cut into chunks
2 tablespoons oil
1 tablespoon vinegar

1. Put all the ingredients, except the venison, liver, oil and vinegar, in a food processor and process until it becomes a purée (add a little water if it gets too thick).

2. Put 4fl oz (110ml) water into a saucepan with the venison and liver and bring to the boil. Turn the heat down, cover and simmer for 15 minutes or until the meat feels almost tender to the fork. Keep to one side, together with any stock.

3. Heat the oil in another saucepan, transfer the meat with a slotted spoon, and fry until brown. Add the spice purée and fry until the oil begins to separate and a delicious aroma rises.

4. Add the vinegar and leftover stock and simmer, covered, until the meat is tender. Add more water if it becomes too dry. Taste and adjust the seasoning.

CORN FRIED PORK

✦

IN BANGKOK, along with vendors selling every type of curry, rice, noodle, satay and stir-fry dish imaginable, there are people sitting in front of huge piles of golden sweetcorn bursting with sweetness and flavour. Buyers point at the cob they want and it is plunged into a vat of continuously boiling water. Then, instead of wrapping the whole cob for them to take away, the vendor makes long sweeping cuts with a wickedly sharp knife and puts the milky kernels into a plastic bag. Alternatively, the customer would take the kernels to the next stall where yet another seller makes this quick and easy dish.

SERVES 4–5

1lb (450g) pork, cut into small cubes
2 tablespoons lard or oil
1 X 14oz (400g) can sweetcorn, drained
4 spring onions, washed, trimmed and
　finely chopped
½ teaspoon salt
4 cloves garlic, peeled and chopped

1 teaspoon sugar
1 tablespoon soy sauce
8oz (225g) French or bobby beans, cut
　into small pieces
½ teaspoon chilli powder (optional)
2 tablespoons finely chopped fresh
　coriander

1. Fry the pork in the lard or oil for 2 minutes until it begins to brown. Add the sweetcorn, spring onions, salt, garlic, sugar, soy sauce and beans, and stir-fry for a few minutes until cooked.

2. Taste and adjust the seasoning (adding more salt or ½ teaspoon chilli powder if liked). Add the chopped coriander, stir, and serve.

BRAISED PORK AND PUMPKIN

✦

WE THINK this marriage of juicy belly of pork with the delicious sweet nuttiness of the pumpkin was made in gourmet heaven. This is welcoming food indeed, and quick and easy to make. No wonder it is a popular Chinese street stall dish.

SERVES 4

2 tablespoons rice wine, mirin or dry sherry
4 tablespoons dark soy sauce
½ teaspoon ground ginger
½ teaspoon ground cinnamon
12oz (350g) belly of pork, cut into ½ inch (1cm) pieces

1 tablespoon oil
1lb (450g) pumpkin, peeled, de-seeded and cut into 2 inch (5cm) cubes
10fl oz (275ml) chicken stock
1 small dried chilli
1 teaspoon sugar

1. Put 1 tablespoon rice wine or sherry in a bowl with 2 tablespoons soy sauce, and the ground ginger and cinnamon. Add the pork and marinate for 2 hours.

2. Heat the oil in a wok and stir-fry the pork for 3 minutes. Then add the pumpkin and stir-fry for a further 2 minutes.

3. Add the stock, chilli, sugar, the marinade and the remainder of the wine or sherry and soy sauce. Bring to the boil, then simmer for 15–20 minutes or until the pork is meltingly tender and the pumpkin is cooked but still holds its shape.

PORK STIR-FRY WITH GREEN BEANS

✦

SHOULDER of pork is one of our favourite cuts when stir-frying or roasting. Long, slow cooking demands a fattier cut, such as belly – ideal for sweet and sour dishes and braising.

Butchers and supermarkets have started selling special 'stir-fry' packs but this puts a hefty premium on the meat. It's more economical to buy one large chunk, save half for roasting and cut the other up for this very easy stir-fry which has a distinctive Malaysian flavour, spicy and warm. It's easier to slice the pork thinly if you put it in the freezer for a few hours beforehand to stiffen.

SERVES 4

2 tablespoons oil
1½lb (675g) pork, thinly sliced
2 cloves garlic, peeled and crushed
2 onions, peeled and thinly sliced
4oz (110g) French or bobby beans, broken into 2 inch (5cm) lengths
1 tomato, cut into 8 pieces
1 teaspoon salt
¼ teaspoon ground black pepper

1 teaspoon ground coriander
½ teaspoon ground cumin
1 teaspoon chilli powder
1 teaspoon vinegar
1 tablespoon oyster sauce
1 teaspoon hoisin sauce or tomato ketchup
1 teaspoon cornflour mixed with 1 teaspoon sherry or ginger wine

1. Heat the oil in a wok and fry the pork over a high heat for 1 minute. Add the garlic and onions, and fry until the onions soften and begin to turn golden (about 3 minutes).

2. Add the beans, tomato, salt, pepper, coriander and cumin and fry for 3 minutes more. Add the rest of the ingredients and mix thoroughly. Cook until the sauce thickens, and serve.

MOULDED PORK IN RICH SPICED GRAVY

✦

THIS IS a Chinese dish with a difference, and it requires a steamer. Serve the sliced meat on a bed of shredded lettuce, with the gravy in a separate dish. Very tender and succulent, this pork dish is also hot and spicy – thanks to the peppercorns. If you can track down Szechuan peppercorns, so much the better.

SERVES 4–6

1 × 1½lb (675g) boneless roasting joint of pork with fat (very important for this dish)

10 tablespoons soy sauce

2 star anise

1 stick cinnamon

2 cloves

3 teaspoons black peppercorns

2 tablespoons sherry

1 tablespoon sugar

1 teaspoon salt

3 spring onions, washed, trimmed and chopped

2 teaspoons cornflour mixed with 2 tablespoons water

1 teaspoon sesame oil

1. Put the pork in a deep saucepan with 8 tablespoons soy sauce, the star anise, cinnamon stick, cloves and peppercorns, and enough water to almost cover the meat. Bring to the boil, cover, then simmer for 1 hour until almost tender. Remove and slice thinly. Reserve the liquid.

2. Arrange the pork in a small heatproof bowl or casserole dish which will fit your steamer. Pour over the remaining soy sauce, sherry, sugar and salt and, lastly, sprinkle the chopped spring onion on the top in a layer.

3. Making sure there is always enough boiling water in your steamer, steam on high for 45 minutes or until the meat is very tender.

4. Strain the liquid the pork was originally boiled in. Put in a saucepan, add the cornflour mixture and boil until thick. Stir in the sesame oil.

5. Unmould and slice the pork carefully and serve the sauce separately.

OPPOSITE Twelve-minute Thai Red Beef Curry (page 106) served with Mango Acharu (page 26) white rice and stir-fried pak choi

OPPOSITE PAGE 115 Arrak Tropical Punch (page 131), Passion Fruit and Mango Ginger Layer (page 121) and Coconut Pancakes (page 123)

Honey-Roasted Pork

✦

ORK STRIPS used to be roasted in large brick ovens in the market squares of ancient China. Now one is more likely to see these delicious honeyed strips rotating in an electric rotisserie mounted on a cart. This is a really easy recipe, which converts a conventional Western oven to an Oriental one. If you can't be bothered with finding meat hooks, the meat can be grilled instead. Tenderloin is the best cut to use but shoulder is equally delicious and economical. Any leftover pork is excellent in soup and other dishes.

Please note that the red colouring found in small plastic containers in Oriental supermarkets is very potent and will dye everything it comes into contact with, including fingers, dishes, serving counters and floor coverings. You have been warned . . . use with great care.

Serves 4–6

1lb (450g) boneless lean pork, cut into 1 inch (2.5cm) × 2 inch (5cm) × 4 inch (10cm) strips

2 tablespoons grated fresh ginger

3 cloves garlic, peeled and crushed

2 spring onions, washed, trimmed and chopped

2 tablespoons hoisin sauce

2 tablespoons dry sherry

4 tablespoons runny honey

2 tablespoons soy sauce

¼ teaspoon ground cinnamon

½ teaspoon red food colouring powder (optional)

1. Put the pork strips in a strong plastic bag with all the ingredients, tie the opening tightly and refrigerate for at least 4 hours or overnight so that all the lovely flavours sink into the meat. Turn the bag occasionally, if you remember.

2. Preheat the oven to 180°C/350°F/Gas Mark 4. Place a roasting tin full of water on the bottom shelf, to help keep the meat moist.

3. Remove all the shelves from the oven except for the top one and the bottom one holding the tray of water. Run a small s-shaped hook through the top of each piece of meat, then hang it from the rungs of the top shelf.

4. Bake at 180°C/350°F/Gas Mark 4 for 30 minutes, then raise the temperature to 230°C/450°F/Gas Mark 8 and bake for another 5–8 minutes or until dark golden brown (or deep browny-red if using colouring). Take out of the oven and slice diagonally.

GOAT CURRY

✦

WHEN WE all lived in Tottenham we sent the kids to a Church of England School and attended Holy Trinity Church opposite the bus garage. The rich mixture of people from all over the world who formed the local community brought their own recipes to church gatherings and we would often hold themed evenings on which we would enjoy food from different regions.

Goat Curry, found throughout the Caribbean and in Muslim countries in the Orient, is one of the best of these dishes. Wherever people migrate they take well-loved recipes with them – that is what makes eating on the streets so exciting! Sadly, goat meat is not very easily available in the UK – if unobtainable, substitute lamb or, even better, mutton.

This curry is quite delicious served over white rice and garnished, if liked, with toasted desiccated coconut, raisins and chopped nuts.

SERVES 6–8

3lb (1.3kg) lean boneless goat meat, cut into 2 inch (5cm) cubes
1 tablespoon vinegar
juice of 1 lime
1 teaspoon salt
1 teaspoon freshly ground black pepper
3 tablespoons oil
2 cloves garlic, peeled and chopped

2 tablespoons curry powder
6fl oz (175ml) chicken stock
1 sprig each of fresh thyme and fresh parsley
1 bay leaf (optional)
2 spring onions, washed, trimmed and chopped
2 medium potatoes, peeled and cubed

1. Put the meat in a dish with the vinegar, lime juice, salt and pepper. Mix well and marinate in the refrigerator for at least 2 hours, turning frequently.

2. Heat the oil in a large pan, fry the garlic until crisp, and then the meat until it browns.

3. Add the curry powder and stir for a few minutes to take away the 'raw' taste. Then add 3fl oz (75ml) water, the stock, herbs and spring onions, and simmer, covered, for about an hour until the meat is almost tender. Add more water if needed.

4. Add the potatoes and simmer again until the potatoes are cooked.

Sweets

I F YOU said to any child, 'I am going to take you to a country where
people will try to give you as much to eat and drink as you want, no one
will ask for your pocket money in return and even your parents will smile as
you scoff on sweets, ice-creams and drinks', what do you suppose would be
the reaction?

But this is exactly what happens during Vesak in Sri Lanka. Vesak is the
most sacred of Buddhist festivals (and the majority of Sri Lankan people
celebrate it). Taking place at full moon in May, Vesak commemorates the
birth, enlightenment and death of the Buddha. Streets are decorated with
the most wonderful paper palaces, animals, cars, geometric shapes – all
made of white tissue paper over bamboo stick supports and many feet tall,
strung up over the road and lit with thousands of little clay coconut oil
lamps.

In the bigger cities, electrically lit *pandals* (panels illustrating events in the
life of Buddha) are strung high across major thoroughfares. Our main interest, though, was in the many *dansals* (food stalls) which dispensed endless
supplies of free food and drink to sightseers and pilgrims alike. The belief is
that benefits come to those who give, so everyone is encouraged to eat and
drink to their hearts' content, especially the children.

This may seem odd to Westerners brought up in a society so geared to the
pursuit of profit and social status. But these are countries where monks
roam the land with nothing but a begging bowl to feed themselves, and
most families have at least one male member spending time in a monastery.
Here, sharing food brings blessings to the giver.

Wander through street markets in South-East Asia and you will see all
sorts of small, dainty-looking sweets, usually wrapped in banana or pandanus leaves. In Thailand, Malaysia and Singapore one finds jelly-like con-
coctions made with coconut milk and tinted green, red and white. They are
disconcertingly salty.

Naturally enough, in Sri Lanka, where coconut palm trees line every coastline, whispering and swaying in the scented breeze, we use coconuts in many ways – in savoury curries, but also for sweets. We used to love buying coconut ice – squares of fresh coconut mixed with condensed milk and sugar – from street traders and our school tuck shop. The coconut ice was brightly coloured. Two amazing colours much beloved by Sri Lankans were *seeni muthi* pink (a particularly violent shocking pink) and a sickeningly bright lime green, and the eye would often be assaulted by this particular combination. We would shut our eyes when eating it, rather than give up one of our favourite sweets.

The following recipes are easily made at home and are among those we bought from street traders on our recent trip.

SHAVED ICE

✦

BOTH DAD (who was brought up in Malaysia) and Chandra's husband John, whose home was Guyana, used to enjoy this childhood treat. The ice man would come around with a huge block of ice in a large tin can. He would use an *adze* (a sort of curved axe) to shave off very thin curls of ice. These would be put into a bowl, and rose sherbet (syrup) flavouring and condensed milk would be drizzled over the top.

SERVES 4

4 tablespoons rose flavouring (from Asian grocery shops) or rose hip syrup (from the chemist)

4 tablespoons condensed milk

1. Put 1 pint (570ml) water in a plastic container and freeze.

2. When almost frozen, whizz in a blender or food processor. Then put back in the freezer.

3. Take the ice out again and use a fork to scrape the top until it looks like drifting snow.

4. Serve in pretty individual glass dishes, with the syrup and milk drizzled over the top.

VARIATIONS

✦ This recipe also works well with other concentrated sweet syrups, such as tangerine, mango and orange, or even apple. Fresh fruit juice is not strong enough.

THALA BALLS

✦

THIS IS a very easy recipe and one of the most famous Sri Lankan sweetmeats. Thala balls are made from a mixture of palm sugar and sesame seeds. If not eaten immediately, the balls or small logs are wrapped in greaseproof paper and the ends twisted, like mini bon-bons or crackers. Every small shop or boutique has a large glass bottle of thala balls on the counter ready to be purchased for a few cents.

Jaggery (palm sugar) can be found in good grocery stores and also at Oxfam shops.

10oz (275g) sesame seeds	1lb (450g) jaggery (palm sugar) or dark
½ teaspoon salt	brown molasses sugar

1. Use a mortar and pestle to pound the sesame seeds, a handful at a time, until oily. Or grind them in an electric coffee grinder.

2. Add the salt and sugar, then turn out onto a work surface and knead until the mixture begins to stick together.

3. Make balls the size of your thumbnail or a 10-pence coin.

4. Store in a cool place and wrap in greaseproof paper if not eaten the same day. Thala balls will keep for up to a week.

PASSION FRUIT AND MANGO GINGER LAYER

✦

SOMETIMES the simplest dishes can be the best. This is our version of a Western recipe. We love the combination of creamy fromage frais mixed with the more Oriental flavours of mango and passion fruit, and it is so easy to make. You can prepare steps 1 and 2 in advance and finish off step 3 at the last moment.

If you are wondering why this dessert is nestling in a book on street food – we ate a similar concoction in Thailand, only it was strangely salty, heavily flavoured with *rampe* (pandanus leaf) and lime water, and made with thick coconut milk. It was oddly synthetic-tasting and not very agreeable to our Westernised palates so we adapted it to suit ourselves and you, we hope.

SERVES 4

8oz (225g) ginger biscuits
2oz (50g) natural (not salted) cashew nuts, toasted in a dry frying pan until golden and roughly chopped
1 × 14oz (400g) can mango slices
2 passion fruit

8oz (225g) fromage frais
1–2 tablespoons runny honey
1 starfruit, thinly sliced
a pinch of ground ginger
whipped cream (optional)

1. Put the biscuits into a food processor and whizz until they form rough crumbs, not too fine. Mix in the cashew nuts. Set aside.

2. Drain the mango slices and put in the processor or blender. Cut the passion fruit in half and add the pulp and seeds, together with the fromage frais and honey, and process until smooth.

3. Take 4 large ice-cream sundae glasses and spoon a layer of crumb mixture into each. Follow with a layer of fruit mixture, and alternate the layers until the glasses are nearly full. Top each one with a slice of starfruit and decorate with a little ground ginger and a whipped cream rose (if liked). Serve immediately.

Starfruit and Lychee Sorbet

✦

ANOTHER easy recipe but gorgeous! It cleans your palate completely so it could be served in between courses at a Chinese banquet. Try accompanying it with small almond biscuits.

Similar sorbets and extra creamy ice-creams used to be sold on South-East Asian streets by people pushing tin barrows or from a tin box strapped to the front of a bicycle. Grandmother would throw up her hands in horror and warn us about the dangers of catching cholera or dysentery but we can't remember ever having even an upset stomach. And don't forbidden fruits always taste the sweetest?! Instead of the tinny strains of 'Greensleeves' which usually emerge from English ice-cream vans, as children we would come running to the sound of the distinctive two-tone klaxon horn.

Starfruit (also known as carambola) is now available in most good supermarkets. Besides being wonderfully decorative when added to fruit salad, it has a sharp, tangy flavour and crispy texture. Choose fruit that is firm and unblemished. In the Far East it is used in savoury chutneys and pickles as well.

Please note that raw egg whites should not be eaten by pregnant women, very small children or the very elderly – in case of salmonella.

SERVES up to 6

2 starfruit
2 × 14oz (400g) cans lychees in syrup
grated rind and 1 teaspoon juice from 1 lime

4 tablespoons caster sugar (or to taste)
4 medium egg whites (free-range or from a reputable source)

1. Wash the starfruit and cut into pieces. Drain the lychees and reserve the juice. Put the starfruit and drained lychees in a food processor and whizz to a purée.

2. Stir in the grated lime rind, lime juice and lychee juice. Add sugar to taste. Turn into a container and freeze until mushy (about 1½–2 hours).

3. Whip the egg whites until stiff, then beat into the ice purée until well blended.

4. Return to the freezer and freeze until solid.

COCONUT PANCAKES

✦

WHEN WE were in Penang we saw street traders making these pancakes throughout the day. Patient queues would form in front of the cook, who would quickly drop some batter onto a flat griddle, deftly spread it with a flat-bladed spatula, then sprinkle a good teaspoon of filling over it, flip one half over, slip the crescent onto a piece of paper and serve it in less time than you or I could make a soft-boiled egg! The green colour came from pandanus leaf (*rampe* in Sri Lanka), squeezed in water, but we use green food colouring with no loss of flavour.

SERVES 4

For the pancakes
1½ pints (900ml) canned coconut milk
6oz (175g) rice flour
3 eggs
4oz (110g) white caster sugar
a pinch of salt
a few drops of green food colouring
   (optional)
1 tablespoon oil
1 oz (25g) melted butter, optional

For the filling
2oz (50g) sesame seeds, toasted
2oz (50g) desiccated coconut (rough cut)
2–3 tablespoons jaggery (palm) or dark
   brown sugar

1. Put all the pancake ingredients, except the oil and melted butter, into a food processor and whizz to make a smooth batter, or beat with a whisk in a large bowl until smooth.

2. Heat a very little oil in a frying pan, and pour in just enough batter to cover the surface.

3. Cook over a medium heat until the bottom is crisp and speckled with brown. Mix all the filling ingredients together, put a little onto the pancake and flip over. Slide onto a warmed plate and serve with melted butter if liked.

VARIATION

✦ Mix 4oz (110g) butter with 1 teaspoon lemon juice, 2 tablespoons white sugar and 2 tablespoons toasted desiccated coconut as an alternative filling.

PAYASAM
Malaysian Milk Pudding

✦

THIS IS about as similar to the dreaded school-dinner milk pudding as chalk is to cheese. Its rich creamy texture, fragrant with Oriental spices, will tempt even confirmed milk pudding haters into trying it – and returning for more.

SERVES 4–5

1oz (25g) angel hair vermicelli
2oz (50g) butter
1½ pints (900ml) milk
a 2 inch (5cm) cinnamon stick
3 cardamom pods, crushed
2 tablespoons white sugar

1oz (25g) chopped almonds, or plain
  cashew nuts, cut into slivers
2 drops almond essence
1 tablespoon sultanas
a pinch of ground turmeric

1. Cut the vermicelli into 2 inch (5cm) lengths and heat the butter in a large heavy-based saucepan. Fry the vermicelli until golden brown, taking care not to scorch it.

2. Add the milk, cinnamon stick, cardamom pods, and sugar. Bring to the boil, then simmer for about 12–15 minutes or until it begins to thicken.

3. Stir in the nuts, almond essence, sultanas and enough turmeric to tint the pudding a delicate primrose, then cook for a further 5 minutes. Serve lukewarm.

GULUB JAMAN
Milk Balls in Syrup

✦

RANI'S friend Usha makes the most heavenly desserts and brings them into work in plastic containers just for her. When life is not going the way Rani wants, one or two (OK, or even more!) of these feather-light, dark-brown balls of milk and flour soaked in a light rose-flavoured syrup convince her that things aren't that bad.

A favourite in most South-East Asian countries – try them and we guarantee they will become one of yours, too.

MAKES 20 balls; enough for 4 greedy people or 6 normal ones!

For the syrup
8oz (225g) white sugar
5 cardamom pods, bruised
2 cloves
1 tablespoon rose water

For the milk balls
1oz (25g) butter

2oz (50g) self-raising flour
4oz (110g) full-cream dried milk powder
1fl oz (25ml) milk, mixed with a pinch of
grated nutmeg (plus a little more milk
if necessary)
1 pint (570ml) oil

1. To make the syrup, put the sugar in a heavy-based saucepan, together with 10fl oz (275ml) water, the cardamom pods, and cloves. Boil, stirring, until the sugar dissolves. Then boil the syrup without stirring until it begins to thicken. Allow to cool slightly, and add the rose water. Leave to cool a little more, before adding the milk balls.

2. To make the milk balls, mix the butter, flour and milk powder together, then add the spiced milk to form a stiff dough. Turn out onto a clean surface and knead well. Form into 24 balls and leave to one side.

3. Heat the oil in a deep saucepan and fry the balls a few at a time, very gently. They will swell before your eyes so you need to allow enough space. Turn in the oil until they go dark brown but do not let them burn. If they split it is either because you didn't spend enough time kneading the mixture or because the oil is too hot. Try again.

4. Drain on kitchen paper and allow to cool.

5. Add the *gulab jaman* balls to the syrup and leave for a couple of hours at least, turning once or twice so that the syrup soaks into the delectable spheres. Serve lukewarm.

GORENG PISANG
Banana Fritters

✦

ON THE streets of South-East Asia the air is spiced with the mouth-watering scents of curries, roasting meats and barbecues, steaming pastries and always the maddening aroma of frying. Every 100 yards or so, a stoical man or woman can be found sitting, stirring a cauldron of boiling oil and fishing out either fish, meat or prawn cakes or, more likely, sweet yam or these banana fritters. There will be an endless queue of people in front of them, for the Thais and Malaysians are particularly fond of this dish.

SERVES 4

4oz (110g) self-raising flour
2oz (50g) rice flour
a pinch of ground cinnamon or cardamom
½ teaspoon salt

1 pint (570ml) oil
4 smallish bananas
icing sugar (optional)
1 lime, cut into wedges (optional)

1. Mix the flours, ground cinnamon or cardamom, and salt together, then add 7fl oz (200ml) water to make a smooth batter. Leave on one side for 30 minutes.

2. Heat the oil in a wok.

3. Peel the bananas and cut each into 2–3 pieces (in the East we would use honey-sweet bananas the size of a baby's finger and fry them whole). Dip into the batter, shake off the excess and fry a few at a time, turning once, until golden brown.

4. Drain on kitchen paper and serve immediately, dusted with icing sugar if liked, and with wedges of fresh lime to squeeze over to counteract the sweetness.

VARIATION

✦ Served with banana ice-cream, this is food for the gods! No banana ice-cream handy? Cheat like we do. Mash 2–3 very ripe bananas and stir into 1¾ pints (1 litre) very good-quality vanilla ice-cream, slightly softened. Return to the freezer to harden. Yummy-scrummy!

WALNUT PUDDING

✦

MOTHER remembers eating this warm, sweet 'soup' between the many courses of a ceremonious banquet in Peking (Beijing). Sometimes served in the same way as the French offer sorbets to cleanse the palate, it can double as a deliciously creamy and nutty pudding.

SERVES 4–6

2 teaspoons oil
1lb (450g) walnuts
8oz (225g) white sugar
⅛ teaspoon salt

a pinch of grated nutmeg
2 tablespoons cornflour mixed to a cream
with 4 tablespoons water

1. Heat the oil in a wok and add the walnuts. Stir-fry until brown, then leave to cool. Take care not to let the nuts burn. When cold, put the nuts in a food processor and grind until very fine.

2. Put all the ingredients, except the cornflour mixture, in a saucepan with 1 pint (570ml) water, and bring to the boil. Simmer for 20 minutes, then add the cornflour and stir until thickened. Allow to cool, then liquidise until absolutely smooth.

VARIATION

✦ Although not strictly authentic, a dollop of cream swirled into this 'soup' served in individual bowls, makes it even more delicious and very pretty.

✦ Instead of walnuts, use a 375g (13 oz) tin of unsweetened chestnut puree – it tastes just as delicious!

Drinks

WE ARE always being asked what one should drink with an Oriental meal. There are some very fine beers brewed in the East – Singha, Elephant, Tiger, Bintag and Anker (these two from Indonesia) and Lion beer come to mind – but a light, fruity, chilled white wine is very acceptable too.

A simple, yet very popular drink which is extremely thirst-quenching is the water from a coconut. Green or Orange (King) coconuts are laid in piles by the wayside. Tender a few coins and someone will whip the top off one with a fierce-looking knife and plunge a straw into it. In Bangkok we saw piles of strange white globes. These turned out to be shelled coconuts which had been steamed. It didn't seem to improve the flavour but they were easier to transport.

Many Oriental drinks are a riot of colour and taste. Some make you wonder if you should drink them or eat them, they are so full of bits of jelly, tapioca, rice, beans, even sweetcorn.

Everywhere you will see industrious hawkers – with mobile pushcarts, market stalls, on bicycles, or just jogging along balancing large baskets on either end of a long bamboo pole. Some of the most delicious drinks are made from the profusion of tropical fruit which is always available. There are mountains of avocados (eaten with sugar and condensed milk, this was one of our childhood favourites); bananas of all sizes and shapes, from the tiny ones about the length of your thumb to big Granddaddy whoppers big enough for two people. And there are less familiar fruits, like papayas, pineapples, rambutans (bright red, with their fierce-looking yet soft bristles concealing incomparably juicy insides), and mangosteens – shiny black orbs with curious purple skins and segmented pure white centres of tart yet sweet heaven.

These are combined with condensed milk or coconut milk, jaggery (palm sugar) syrup, and various sweet fruit syrups to make all sorts of delicious drinks.

Arrack, Sri Lanka's favourite spirit, is also found in Indonesia and

Malaysia. Made from the fermented sap of coconut flowers, it is lethal to the unsuspecting, and tastes similar to brandy. Drunk fresh, it is called toddy.

Here are some of our favourite drinks recipes, cadged from relatives and reeking of the last days of the Raj. You can almost hear the creaking of the large palm fans which would be operated by a series of ropes and pulleys tied to the foot of a bored *punka wallah* or fan boy!

Sipping one of these long drinks (decorated with fresh fruit and flowers), while watching the sun go down, must rank as one of the best experiences on earth. Should you ever be fortunate enough to watch a sunset over Mount Lavinia beach, Sri Lanka, you will be blessed indeed. The sun is a gigantic ball of angry orange and, as it begins to sink, it tints the surrounding sky with Gauguin-like splashes of green, red, orange, yellow, blue – bright primary colours belonging to the paintbox of some giant's child. The sun hangs against this vivid backdrop, then plummets down, and you almost can hear the hiss as it seems to hit the deep ebony sea. The sky rapidly darkens and night falls. If you haven't watched a tropical moon rising you haven't lived – book your flight now!

MILK PUNCH

♦

A DECEPTIVELY mild name for a drink that, taken to excess, will lay you out as surely as a mule's kick! Arrack is made from distilled coconut flowers' sap. It is a beautiful mellow golden brown in colour and tastes similar to a good Napoleon brandy, Scotch or Bourbon. See if you can track it down at a specialist Oriental grocer's.

SERVES 1

4–5 ice cubes
1 teaspoon jaggery (palm) or brown sugar
2 parts arrack or Scotch

3 parts milk
a pinch of ground nutmeg

1. Put the ice cubes in a cocktail shaker with the sugar, arrack or whisky and milk.

2. Shake until a frost forms, then pour into a highball glass (medium-sized tumbler).

3. Sprinkle the nutmeg on top and serve.

ARRACK TROPICAL PUNCH

✦

WHEN WE were children, if Dad had to stay late in the office we used to go home on the school bus. On the way home to Nugegoda, a suburb of Colombo, we would pray for traffic jams at one particular spot. Then, balanced precariously, someone holding our legs, we would reach out of the top deck windows and pluck mangoes from the wayside trees – scrumping Asian-style! This recipe is one of the many in which we later learned to use this wonderful fruit.

SERVES 1

½ large ripe mango, peeled, stoned and
    diced
juice of 1 fresh lime
1 teaspoon sugar (or to taste)
3 parts arrack, rum or brandy

6 ice cubes
1 slice fresh orange
1 slice fresh lime
1 slice fresh lemon

1. Whizz the mango to a purée in a blender. Then put all the ingredients, except the ice and fruit slices, in a jug, stir and leave in the refrigerator for 3 hours.

2. Put the ice cubes in a clean tea towel, then bash them with a rolling pin.

3. Fill a lowball (small whisky) glass with the crushed ice and pour the punch over.

4. Decorate with twists of orange, lime and lemon, finished with a small fresh flower on top.

BANANA HEAVEN

✦

EVERYONE grows at least two or three banana plants in their gardens back home. As soon as the bananas are harvested and the plant cut down, lo and behold, another one springs up close to the mother plant, making this the easiest and most economical fruit crop to grow. When fed up with Banana Fritters (p.126), banana curry, banana cake and banana bread, you can always drink the damn things!

SERVES 1

1 part cream
1 large ripe banana, peeled and cut into
  chunks

3 parts brandy
½ teaspoon sugar (or to taste)
4–5 ice cubes

1. Put all the ingredients, except the ice cubes, in a liquidiser and whizz until smooth.

2. Put the ice cubes in a clean tea towel, then bash them with a rolling pin.

3. Put the crushed ice in a tall glass, and pour over the creamy drink.

Lime Juice

✦

WHEN temperatures soar into the 90s or even higher, there is nothing quite like a refreshing cordial served over crushed ice. This recipe is really delicious. Try freezing it until almost frozen, then whizzing in a liquidiser until slushy. Serve in a long glass with a spoon and straw. Mmmm . . . !

Serves 3

4 limes   ice cubes
4oz (110g) brown sugar (or to taste)

1. Grate the rind of 1 lime, then squeeze all 4 limes.

2. Put the rind, juice and sugar in a jug with 1 pint (570ml) water, and stir until the sugar dissolves.

3. Put the ice cubes in a clean tea towel, then bash them with a rolling pin.

4. Put plenty of crushed ice in each glass, pour over the lime cordial, and serve.

MELON SQUASH

✦

MELONS come in so many shapes, colours and sizes, all with a sweetness and intoxicating fragrance of their own. This is a super drink which is fragrant and thirst-quenching and so pretty!

SERVES 2–3

2 large slices watermelon
1 large slice melon (any kind or a mixture
  of several)
juice of 1 lime
1 tablespoon ginger wine
½ teaspoon brandy (optional)

2–3 ice cubes
ginger ale
a pinch of ground ginger
2–3 fresh mint leaves

1. Scoop some of the melon into balls and reserve for decoration. Dice the rest, discarding the seeds. Then whizz the melon chunks in a blender.

2. Put the liquidised melon into a jug, add the lime juice, ginger wine and brandy if liked. Stir, then refrigerate for about 3 hours or until ice cold.

3. Pour into tall glasses over a cube of ice, and fill to the brim with cold ginger ale. Sprinkle with the ground ginger and garnish with a fresh mint leaf and melon balls.

VARIATION

✦ This makes a delicious sorbet too. Freeze the mixture (without the ginger ale) and, when it becomes mushy, beat with a fork. Refreeze, then repeat, whisking the slush until it becomes a soft ice. Freeze again. Serve in small portions, with a good crisp biscuit.

SINGAPORE SLING

✦

NOBODY travels to Singapore without at least trying to visit the world-famous Raffles Hotel, that pinnacle of high living where waiters whisper and wear white cotton gloves. And even fewer (except those who are sworn teetotallers) can resist ordering a Singapore Sling. The hotel's recipe is a jealously guarded secret, but this is our version. Serve in an ice-cold collins glass (large straight-sided tumbler).

A word of warning: This excellent thirst-quencher for a hot summer's day tastes so innocuous it is quite easy to render oneself or one's guests totally legless, so beware!

SERVES 2

12–16 ice cubes
juice of 1 lemon
juice of 1 orange
2 tablespoons crushed pineapple
2 parts cherry brandy
6 parts gin

6 drops Angostura bitters
2 slices fresh orange
2 slices fresh lemon
soda water
2 cocktail cherries

1. Mix 1 serving at a time. Put 4–5 ice cubes in a cocktail shaker with half the fruit juices, crushed pineapple, cherry brandy, gin and bitters.

2. Shake hard until a frost forms.

3. Put 2 more ice cubes in the glass, pour over the mixture and garnish with the fruit slices.

4. Carefully top with soda water, pop a cherry on top, and serve.

PASSION FRUIT COOLER

✦

THE PASSION flower is a very pretty creeping plant with feathery curling fronds, beautiful flowers (said to resemble Jesus' crown of thorns), and small round fruits like wizened brownish-purple apples that produce a pulp of delicious flavour. This drink is ambrosia indeed.

SERVES 3

4 passion fruit
4 slices canned pineapple

4oz (110g) white sugar (or to taste)
ice cubes

1. Cut the passion fruit in half and scoop out all the pulp and seeds.

2. Put the pulp and seeds, pineapple, sugar and 1 pint (570ml) water in a liquidiser and whizz until blended.

3. Put the ice cubes in a clean tea towel and bash them with a rolling pin.

4. Put plenty of crushed ice in 3 tall glasses, pour over the passion fruit cooler, and serve.

LASSI

✦

NO ORIENTAL cookbook is complete without a recipe for lassi. Totally thirst-quenching and designed to dampen a too-hot curry, lassi is a healthy alternative to alcohol. Dad used to suffer from the sweetest tooth in the family but also had diabetes. So he learned to drink, and like, salty lassi and swore by its refreshing qualities.

SERVES 3–4

10fl oz (275ml) plain yoghurt
either 2 teaspoons salt and a pinch of
   ground turmeric *or* 1 tablespoon white
   sugar and a little rose or orange water

ice cubes
a few mint leaves

1. Put the ingredients (except the ice cubes and mint leaves) in a blender, together with 10fl oz (275ml) water, and whizz until well-mixed and frothy.

2. Pour over the ice cubes and decorate with the mint leaves.

VARIATION
✦ Mint lassi has quite a different taste. Instead of adding rose or orange water, add 4–5 mint leaves to the liquidiser and a drop of peppermint essence (optional).

ICED COFFEE

✦

W E COULD not leave this recipe out, for at every family 'do' long glasses of iced coffee would be handed out, together with sticky date cake and birthday cake. Birthdays are particularly special occasions for Sri Lankans and *everyone* is invited. It is quite common for 50 to 100 people to turn up even at a children's party.

The men would generally congregate outside to smoke, drink and tell rude jokes. (As children, we could never hear the punchlines, no matter how hard we strained our ears.) Women and children would be inside, in the cool of the air-conditioned rooms doing whatever we were supposed to do, i.e. discuss the latest fashions, gossip about anyone silly enough not to have turned up, bicker and play games. We're sorry if this sounds terribly sexist but that's what we did!

SERVES 3–4

10fl oz (275ml) very strong black coffee
7fl oz (200ml) sweetened condensed milk
½ teaspoon ground cardamom

½ teaspoon vanilla essence
full-cream milk (to taste)
ice cubes

1. Mix the coffee, condensed milk, ground cardamom and vanilla essence together and whisk until frothy.

2. Add milk to taste. Serve well chilled over ice cubes.

VARIATION

✦ We remember that some of our family cooks used to add a raw egg and a pinch of grated nutmeg to this recipe. Chandra swears she could taste the minutest quantity but then she hates runny eggs (she cooks fried eggs to concrete for her family) and advocaat, while Rani's adolescent drink was a frothy snowball, crowned with the obligatory cherry – how sad!

Glossary

Allspice – Also known as Jamaican pepper, this fragrant berry combines the flavours of cinnamon, nutmeg and cloves in one spice. Equally good in savoury or sweet dishes.

Arrack – Sri Lanka's best-loved alcoholic drink, made from the fermented sap of coconut flowers; also found in Indonesia and Malaysia. The unfermented version is known as toddy.

Bamboo Shoots – Rather bland in taste, like bean curd, bamboo shoots have a chameleon-like ability to absorb seasonings, and add a delicious crunch to stir-fries and braised dishes. Widely available in canned form, they need to be drained before use.

Beansprouts – These are the shoots of sprouted mung beans. If stir-frying beansprouts, cook them for no more than a couple of minutes to retain their crispness. They also make a welcome addition to salads.

Bean Curd/Tofu – Made from puréed yellow soya beans, tofu is essentially tasteless but possesses high protein value. It is sold in the form of white gelantinous cakes covered in water, and can be added to meat, fish or vegetables where it will absorb all the flavours of the dish. It can also be coated in rice or cornflour, fried and added to other dishes or it can be eaten by itself with dipping sauces.

Besan gram Flour/Chickpea Flour – Especially good to make batter for coating deep-fried foods, as it sticks like glue.

Blachan/Shrimp Paste – Often used to give the familiar fish undertone to South-East Asian dishes, this paste is made of dried shrimps and possesses a very strong odour. If the paste is wrapped in kitchen foil and baked in the oven for approximately 10 minutes, it blends more easily with other ingredients. Use sparingly.

Black Beans – Salted soya beans commonly used to add a distinctive flavour to Chinese dishes. Should be soaked for 10 minutes before use to remove excess salt, then mashed to release maximum flavour.

Cardamom – These fragrant little black seeds are encased in small green, white or black-coloured pods. They can be used whole or the seeds can be extracted from the pods before cooking. Usually added to give depth to curries and braised dishes. Also frequently used in cakes and sweets in the East or as a breath-freshener. We refer throughout the book to green cardamom pods.

Chillies – A common ingredient in Sri Lankan, Indian and Thai cuisine, chillies come in a variety of colours and shapes, fresh and dried, pieces and powdered. The general rule is that the smaller the chilli, the hotter the taste! The heat is provided by the seeds in the chilli pod and these can be removed from fresh chillies if a milder taste is required.

Cinnamon – The bark of the cinnamon tree produces this fragrant spice which is used equally in savoury and sweet dishes in the East.

Cloves – The pungent aromatic dried buds of a tropical tree, available whole or in powdered form. Only a small amount is required to add a subtle tone to savoury or sweet dishes.

Coconut Milk/Cream – In Sri Lanka the flesh of the coconut is grated and mixed with a very small amount of warm water to obtain the thick milk known as coconut cream. The same pulp can then be squeezed again, twice more, to make a thinner liquid known as coconut milk. Coconut milk is widely available in powder or block form (known as creamed coconut), which has to be mixed with hot water to get the consistency required. It can also be found ready-to-use in cans. Desiccated coconut is well known to Western cooks, usually for cake-making.

Coriander – The main spice in most curries when mixed with cumin and turmeric. Also known as *dhania*, coriander can be found as seeds, powder or as fresh leaves. The seeds can be used whole or ground, and a stronger flavour is gained by dry-roasting them for 2–3 minutes over a medium heat in a heavy-based pan until they darken in colour. The fresh leaves are also known as Chinese parsley. Fresh coriander should be kept refrigerated in a plastic bag and is easily grown at home from the seeds. Substituting dried coriander for fresh will not give the same flavour; ordinary parsley should be used in recipes if fresh coriander cannot be found.

Cumin – Cumin seeds can be used whole, ground or roasted in the same way as coriander seeds. Sometimes roasted ground cumin is sprinkled on top of cooked dishes as a final flavouring.

Curry Leaves – Also known as *karapincha* in Sri Lanka, curry leaves are an important element in Asian cooking. A few leaves added to any dish will impart a delicate curry smell and flavour. The leaves can be fried and crumbled into dishes for a more robust taste. There is no alternative.

Dhal – Lentils or pulses cooked with spices and served with rice or breads. A nourishing vegetarian alternative to meat.

Fennel – The flavouring agent used in liquorice. Extremely good with meat dishes to impart a sweet, fragrant flavour.

Fenugreek – These yellow seeds accentuate the flavour of lighter spices. Particularly good with vegetables, the seeds are slightly bitter and should be used sparingly.

Fish Sauce – Also known as *nam pla* in Thailand, *patis* in the Philippines, and *nuoc mam* in Vietnam, Laos and Kampuchea. Made from pressed salted anchovies, this thin brown liquid is often used instead of salt in South-East Asian cuisine.

Five Spice Powder – A mixture of five spices, ground to a powder, commonly used in Chinese cooking. Consists of star anise, fennel seeds, cinnamon, Szechuan pepper and cloves. The pretty flower-like star anise provides the distinctive aniseed smell and flavour of this mixture. There is also an Indian version of five spice powder which consists of equal quantities of cumin, mustard seed, star anise, nigella and fenugreek.

Galangal – A member of the ginger family, galangal is used extensively in South-East Asian cooking. Pound in a mortar and pestle, grinder or liquidiser with a little water. The dried form of galangal requires soaking before it can be treated as above.

Garlic – Along with ginger and onions, garlic forms the 'trinity' required for most Oriental and Asian cuisine. The medicinal properties of garlic are now well known and fresh garlic, puréed garlic, dried garlic flakes and powdered garlic are widely available.

Ghee – Clarified butter used for cooking foods at high temperatures where ordinary butter would burn. Easily made by melting butter and separating the clear clarified butter from the residue.

Ginger – This aromatic root provides a warm, spicy note in savoury or sweet dishes. Fresh ginger should be peeled and grated, or liquidised with a little water in a blender or food processor, before use. Can also be found in dried powder form although this is not in the same class as fresh ginger. Ginger can be stored in the refrigerator, wrapped in cling film, or buried in sandy soil where it will not only retain its freshness but will produce more shoots for use, if it is sparingly watered.

Hoisin Sauce – A thick sweetish-brown sauce made of soya beans, garlic, chilli and spices. Especially good for flavouring barbecues and grills.

Jaggery – Brown sugar made from palms. Used commonly in Sri Lanka in place of cane sugar and, mixed with coconut, it is the basis of many Sri Lankan puddings and sweets. If jaggery (palm sugar) is not readily available, dark brown sugar can be substituted (the addition of a little maple or golden syrup improves the flavour).

Kaffir Lime Leaves – Often used in Thai dishes, these leaves add the distinctive aroma of lime. If unavailable, grated lime rind may be substituted.

Lemon Grass – A grasslike plant which imparts a delicate citrus flavour. Extensively used in Thai and Sri Lankan cuisine. Grated lemon rind can be substituted but will have a stronger flavour.

Lentils or Pulses – Also known as *dhal*, these are packed with protein and are the staple food of many households in the East. There are many different types of lentils, the commonest being *moong dhal* (the green whole grain is the mung bean used for beansprouts, whilst the yellow type is hulled and split), *urid dhal* (black is the whole grain; white is split and hulled) and *channa dhal* (a branch of the split pea family and considerably larger than *moong dhal*). It is believed that the addition of asafoetida when cooking lentils reduces the unfortunate side-effect of eating too many pulses – flatulence!

Maldive Fish – An essential ingredient of many Sri Lankan dishes, maldive fish is indigenous to the Maldive Islands, after which it is named. Flakes of this dried fish are used, like fish sauce in Thailand, to add a light fishy undertone to many dishes. If unavailable, ground dried shrimps are an acceptable alternative.

Mirin – Available from Oriental food shops, mirin is a sweet Japanese wine made from rice. Sweet sherry or white wine are acceptable alternatives.

Mushrooms – The Chinese use a wide variety of mushrooms in cooking, from button mushrooms to wood ear and straw mushrooms. Wood ears are a dried fungus and should be soaked for 20 minutes in water, drained, rinsed and have their stems removed before being sliced and cooked. Straw mushrooms are usually sold in cans and should be drained before use. They have a special affinity with crab dishes. Both these mushrooms are used to add texture rather than taste, as they are quite bland in flavour.

Mustard Oil – Unsaturated oil obtained from mustard seeds. Commonly used to flavour dishes from India (especially around Bengal) and Sri Lanka. Usually available from Asian food stores.

Mustard Seeds – Commonly found as black or yellow seeds, used to add a pungency to many Asian dishes. Can be used whole or ground in a mortar and pestle or a coffee grinder.

Nutmeg – Although usually sold in powdered form, fresh nutmeg should be used for preference, stored in an airtight jar, and grated as required. The outer covering of the nutmeg is known as mace and this is exceptionally good in green vegetable dishes.

Oil – The best types of oils to use when cooking Oriental food are those which are not too highly flavoured, such as vegetable, sunflower and corn oil. Olive oil is never used in authentic Oriental dishes, as it is too strongly flavoured and is an uncommon ingredient in the East.

Oyster Sauce – A thick brown sauce made from oyster extract, sugar, soy sauce and spices, often used in Chinese cooking. Flavours vegetables particularly well.

Pak Choi/Bok Choy – A type of Chinese lettuce which is freely available for sale in Chinese supermarkets and easily grown at home from seeds, as long as it is well watered. The delicate flavour of this long green leaf, with its white central stalk, enhances many recipes and requires a minimum of cooking. Chinese greens (e.g. *choi sam*) and Chinese cabbage are also sometimes known as *pak choi*. If unavailable, cos lettuce would make an inferior alternative.

Pandanus Leaves – This member of the screwpine family is also known as *rampe* in Sri Lanka. Used frequently in South-East Asia to flavour and colour dishes from curry to cakes. The flavour is so delicate that we believe it can be omitted altogether without affecting the dish too substantially. The light green colour it imparts to cakes and desserts can be achieved by the lightest touch of well-diluted green food colouring.

Sesame Seeds – The seeds of this annual herbaceous tropical plant are used in both savoury and sweet dishes. The seeds can be roasted in a dry non-stick pan (for only a few seconds, as they burn in the wink of an eye) for a stronger flavour. Sesame oil is used for flavouring cooked dishes but rarely used undiluted for cooking, as it also burns very easily.

Sherry – Dry sherry is an acceptable substitute in dishes requiring rice wine.

Shrimp Paste – See **Blachan**.

Soy Sauce – An essential ingredient in Chinese cuisine, soy sauce comes in a light or dark variety. The light soy sauce is more commonly used in stir-frying, while the dark variety is used to impart a richer flavour to braised and slow-cooked dishes.

Starfruit – Also known as carambola, starfruit is now widely available in the larger supermarkets. Light green on the outside when young, it has a sharp citrus flavour which becomes sweeter as it ripens and turns a sunny yellow. It is particularly decorative because the fruit, as its name implies, is shaped like a star.

Sticky/Glutinous Rice – A white rice which becomes transparent and sticky when cooked. Both the rice, and the flour obtained from it, are often used in sweet dishes.

Tamarind – A velvety fruit pod, the liquid from the pulp is used to add a distinctive sweet/sour note to dishes. Most commonly found in dried block form, the juice can be extracted by soaking a 2 inch (5cm) piece in enough hot water to cover, leaving it for 30 minutes, then squeezing the pulp and straining the liquid before use. The residue of seeds and pulp is discarded.

Turmeric – The poor man's saffron, this hard yellow root gives a golden hue to dishes when used in powder form. Careful handling is required when using turmeric, as anything it comes into contact with may be stained a fetching shade of bright yellow.

Tung Choi – This is Chinese preserved cabbage and garlic shoots, known by a variety of names: Tianjin preserved vegetable (made from Tianjin cabbage), winter cabbage pickle or *tung tsai*. These savoury, salty, brownish flakes of preserved vegetable are usually sold in sachets or lovely little earthenware pottery jars. An invaluable addition to the storecupboard, *tung choi* can be used to give additional flavour to soups, fried rice, noodles, meat or bland vegetable dishes.

Index